Foxdown Wood

Foxdown Wood is under threat from unscrupulous property developers, and Matt and Cathy are determined to save the ancient wood and its wildlife. Then they are unexpectedly summoned to the Other World—a place that is somehow familiar, but also very unlike their own. It seems that each world's struggles between good and evil are linked in some way—but can the children do anything to help?

Beth Webb lives in Somerset with her four children and an entourage of pets. Her stories are mostly based on real places or events, intertwined with traditional folk legends. This, she says, is a good excuse for going out somewhere nice for the day and taking a book of old tales to read.

Beth Webb's other children's books for Lion Publishing are *The Magic in the Pool of Making*, *The Dragons of Kilve* and *Fleabag and the Ring Fire*.

To Phil, Rosie, 'Bud Goode' and all my friends at 'Knapsden'. My thanks.

Foxdown Wood

Beth Webb

A LION BOOK

Text copyright © 1997 Beth Webb
This edition copyright © 1997 Lion Publishing

The author asserts the moral right to be
identified as the author of this work

Published by
Lion Publishing plc
Sandy Lane West, Oxford, England
ISBN 0 7459 3848 5

First edition 1997
10 9 8 7 6 5 4 3 2 1 0

A catalogue record for this book
is available from the British Library

Printed and bound in Great Britain by Caledonian

Acknowledgments
Thanks to John Ralls for asking me to write a story
about a boy and a fox, and Cathy Patterson for telling
me about chewing-gum sandwiches, and lending me
her name! My thanks, also, to Mr Stephen Minnitt of
the Somerset County Museums Service for his advice,
to Brian Penney for suggesting I include Duke, and to
Phil, Rosie and 'Bud Goode' Bird for welcoming me to
'Knighthayes Cottage'.

Contents

The 1 Fox

The small vixen lifted the stump of her forepaw. It was aching. It always did when her Other World was close.

She turned her head and sniffed the air. Car fumes, but different ones from usual.

She ran uncomfortably to the small knoll from where she could see Boy's house. There was indeed a strange car down there, and two female humans. A woman and a girl. There was something about one of them that made the vixen's paw ache even more. Something she recognized, although she was certain she had never smelled either of them before... But she was too far away to be sure.

The young fox watched as best she could without breaking her cover of coppiced hazel. The two humans walked up the path, but they didn't go to see Boy. They went next door, to the empty house, the house that stood where the gate to King Methwin's lodge would be in that Other World, so far away, yet so near.

Ah, Methwin's Land! It was only a short run to get to

it. There it would be warm and summery, rich and welcoming—yet at the same time deadly dangerous. There, everything was clear to her, and she understood speech and could make words like a human. There she was welcomed by the King himself!

But, sadly, she never felt she could explain to the King what he needed to know. She was only a timid creature who watched everything and understood little. But Methwin was never angry with her. He listened to what she said, fed her well, and asked her to come again soon.

However, wonderful as the Other World was, the vixen never felt at home there. Somehow, despite the dangers, cold and hunger of Foxdown Wood she was always glad to come back. Here, she was an ordinary animal like any other—dumb, timid, and with a missing forepaw, limping through the undergrowth and hiding in an old badger's set, dependent on Boy to care for her.

This was where she belonged, and she knew Boy needed her as much as she needed him. The dog food Boy brought when he could was better than grubbed-up worms or dead birds. Since she had caught her front paw in a snare, she could not hunt or dig for her own food properly. Without Boy, she knew she would be dead. Boy was good to her. He had rescued her from the snare. He had brought her here, where she felt safe.

If she had known the words, she would have said Boy loved her, and she loved him.

'One day,' she thought, 'I will take Boy to the Other World. I would like to speak to him and show him what it's like there. He might be able to give the King the answers he needs as to why his world is in such danger.'

She wasn't sure whether she dared do it. Would Boy be able to get there in the same way she could? Would Methwin or the Guardian of the Wood be angry? Dare she trust a human? Boy had saved her life. He always looked after her. He was her friend... Wasn't he?'

But then she had a dreadful thought: 'Boy might get hurt in one of the battles between Methwin and his nephew Harawed... Methwin might not *want* humans in his land... She would not dare to risk it. The fields and woods where the humans lived were intertwined with the Other World like dodder on a bramble. Perhaps Boy would find his own way there one day. Perhaps the Guardian would summon him there as he had once summoned her...'

The noise of angry human voices arguing brought the fox back to the present. She blinked her wide, amber eyes as she scanned the scene below.

The humans were shouting. The girl was throwing bundles and packages onto the middle of the path, and kicking them. She snatched something from the woman and disappeared around the side of the house. The fox's sharp hearing heard a door creaking open. 'What would they find there? Would it be as grand and rich and welcoming inside as Methwin's home? Was it, too, a gateway to the Other World—one that humans could go through?'

The fox watched the two humans disappear inside. How she wished she weren't so timid and dared go with them to see what they saw...

Knighthayes Cottage

The vixen would have been disappointed. The little redbrick cottage was nothing like King Methwin's Hall. There were no sumptuous tapestries, no freshly swept floors strewn with dried reeds and meadow-herbs. There was no green-mantled king to greet them.

In fact, when Cathy Mackeson managed to force open the stiff, swollen front door of the cottage, the first thing she saw was...

MICE!!

Mice everywhere!

Little brown ones with minute, beady eyes. They shot out from right under her feet! Cathy liked mice and was intrigued. She pushed the door open a little further against the deep pile of yellowed newspapers and curled 'special offer' leaflets. More mice ran out followed by...

THE BIG BLACK AND HAIRIES!!

Huge, swollen-bellied spiders with enormously long whiskery legs.

Cathy did *not* like spiders! She gasped and sprang back against her mother who was standing right behind her.

'I am *not* going in there with those... those... *man-eating tarantulas!* Not for anything. You can't *make* me go in there. I'm going home!' And she turned and marched back down the path, ducking the prickly branches that stretched in her way.

Cathy's mother gave another shove against the door to open it fully, and walked in through the paper-strewn lobby to the sitting-room. It was dark inside, although it was only late afternoon. She picked her way between the bits of furniture and opened the curtains.

She looked out of the window at her daughter sulkily hanging over the gate at the end of the path. Poor girl, she couldn't go anywhere else. There was nowhere else to go, except to relatives they really didn't like. An old friend had loaned them the cottage rent-free, provided they cleaned it up a bit. No one had lived there for a couple of years, and it looked like it! Romantically called Knighthayes Cottage, the name couldn't have been further from the truth. There were no knights in armour to look after them, no servants to sweep the floor and bring refreshments.

Cathy's mother smiled to herself as if she were half-remembering something wonderful from long ago. Then she turned and leaned against the window-sill as she surveyed the room, trying to be practical. The rays of late afternoon sun struggled with the dirt on the window and won in the end, leaving golden patches on the walls and floor and giving the room a pleasant air. But it would need a lot of work to make this feel anything like a home for them both.

'Oh, Maggie!' she said to herself. '*How* are you going to sort this one out?' She shook her head in despair. Perhaps it wouldn't have been so bad if there *had* been something remotely knightly or magical about it, but there wasn't. The cottage was a dump, and they were both miserable and intensely lonely.

Poor Cathy. She had been a happy, ordinary girl, just coming to the end of middle school before this all happened. Everything had seemed so nice and comfy at home until...

But this was no time to be thinking about the past.

Maggie found the electric meter at the back of a smelly cupboard in the kitchen. This side of the house had no sun, and was gloomy and dreary. She turned the power on, unsure whether she really wanted to see the room in the light—things might look even worse. She stared at the corpse of a blackbird in the corner. She didn't relish the idea of sleeping in the cottage any more than her daughter did. They would just have to sleep in the car tonight.

She picked up her handbag and stepped outside, pulling the door firmly behind her. 'Come on!' she announced, with as much cheer as she could muster. 'We'll go down to that chippy we spotted and dine in style tonight!'

'How about we go home?' Cathy muttered, under her breath. Then out loud she said defiantly, 'I'm not hungry!' And, turning her back on her mother, she swung violently on the gate like a six-year-old.

Her Mum sighed and hung her head, but walked steadfastly out into the road, taking a few paces towards the shops. No amount of reasoning would help. Cathy knew all the ins and outs. They had all been rehearsed endlessly. Dad didn't want to live with them any more, and they couldn't afford to stay in the old house on their own. There was no point saying anything to Cathy. She would only wag her head from side to side and chant the words back at her.

Mum turned back and looked at her daughter. She said firmly, but as kindly as possible, ' Well, *I'm* going to the chippy. You can stay here—or you can come along, whichever you like.' And, with that, she continued walking. Cathy was behind her in a trice, but her mood was as thick as beeswax, making her face tight and sullen.

After a little while Mum tried to make conversation. 'It was nice of Linda to lend us the cottage, wasn't it? I mean, rent-free and everything.'

Silence.

'Well, we'd have had to have stayed with the Aunts, otherwise...' Cathy suppressed a shiver at the mention of 'the Aunts', two fearsome old harridans who lived in Bexhill-on-Sea, terrorizing everyone—everyone, that is, except their beloved peke who was pampered to within an inch of its life.

'I can't see why we couldn't have stayed at home with Dad!' she blurted out. She knew she was being difficult, but she did wish they hadn't left Norwich. Her friend Rebekah was beaten by her Dad quite often and her family didn't leave him, so why did they have to leave their nice, quiet, friendly Dad, who said that he loved her? It didn't make sense. She glanced at her Mum. Cathy knew she was crying by the way her shoulders were twitching, but she didn't care.

In fact she didn't care at all. 'If you must know, I think your so-called 'cottage in the country' is

CRUMMY! I don't like it, I won't stay there, and I want to go home. I think your precious friend Linda let you have it free because even the fleas have left in disgust!'

And, with that, she flounced into the chip shop and ordered the most expensive thing on the menu. She did not want it. She was not hungry, but with any luck if she asked for too much, Mum would run out of money, then they would *have* to go back. Then everything would be all right, even though she knew nothing would ever be the same again.

A few minutes later, Cathy stormed out of the chip shop, clutching the warm, steamy package to her chest as she strode quickly ahead, all the way back to the cottage.

She ran up the path, ducking the tangle of dog-roses, and turned the corner to go in the back door which they had found opened more easily than the front one. Just as she began struggling with the latch, she caught sight of a ginger mop of hair and two scowling eyes peering down at her from a bedroom window next door. Impulsively, she stuck out her tongue. She did not care what the new neighbours thought of her. In fact, she would feel better if they *did* hate her. They'd 'have words' with Mum, and then Mum would be too embarrassed to stay and they'd have to go back...

Cathy paused and stared at the large, piercing eyes still staring at her from behind the neighbour's immaculately clean window-pane. The eyes seemed to have widened in what could have been amazement, and a freckled, snub nose had joined the right cheek and forehead squashed against the glass.

But she didn't care.

Next door, Matt sat back on his haunches and pulled his duvet over his shoulders. 'Well!' he said aloud to himself, 'We'll have to get rid of Miss Fat Tongue, and quickly!'

Boy

3

Matt waited until it was almost dark. He pulled on his Dad's black anorak and tugged the hood over his face to hide his shock of ginger hair. There was only half an hour before he was supposed to be in bed. He had to be quick and he must not be seen. He grabbed a tin of dog food, opened it, pierced the jellified contents with a fork, and ran.

He was fairly confident that his precautions were unnecessary. From the sounds coming from next door, the tired-looking woman and her rude daughter were too busy cleaning and arguing to worry about one more shadow in their garden.

By skirting the plum and damson trees at the end of the garden, then avoiding the slimy pond on his right, Matt knew he could be in the wood within seconds. He could keep this up for another week or so, but as summer came on, the light would linger well past his bedtime, and he would not be able to take this short cut. It was only fifteen strides across the next-door garden, compared with the twenty-minute walk each way if he went by the road. He moved swiftly, knowing every treacherous bough and tree root. He was angry this evening. He could taste the anger in his mouth. This was *his* garden. He had taken possession of its wilderness when the last tenants had moved out. Surely he had earned some common-law right of way in that time?

Pushing the rusty barbed wire aside with the back of his arm, Matt slithered under the vicious spikes. Holding the dog food carefully, he rustled through the damp grass and up the bank on the other side. Here he felt lighter—freer—almost as if he were in another world far from the pettiness and irritations of his own. For this was Foxdown Wood.

In two or three more minutes he had climbed the hill topped by the leafy knoll, where the vixen had hidden to watch the newcomers earlier that afternoon. Matt could smell her presence. He turned his back on his home and on the long ribbon of raggle-taggle houses that made up the village of Knapsden. Instead, he gazed across the fields that straggled the lower slopes of the Chilterns, chalky and glowing almost pale blue with ultra-violet white in the late evening air. The wood itself was not large, mostly silver birch and beech, dotted with a few portly oaks and some ancient coppiced hazel left to go wild. The whole wood was only the size of a couple of football pitches, but it was special, it was *his* place, and it was where Vix, his only real friend, lived.

Matt sat down under an oak, cupped his hands around his mouth and made a low coughing-barking sound a few times. Soon there was a rustling noise and a small shadow hobbled to his side.

Matt spoke a few words very softly, but he did not

touch or stroke the animal's wiry hair. The vet who had
amputated the vixen's paw had said that if she was
going to survive in the wild, she must not become too
tame. As little contact as possible was the rule. She
must never trust humans.

Matt knew he shouldn't even speak to her, but he
was so lonely, he had to talk to someone and Vix was
ideal, she wouldn't go and blab to his Dad about what
he had said. The boy longed to push his fingers
through the animal's thick coat and scratch the soft
underhairs very gently. Most of all, he longed to put his
arms around her small, strong body and rub his face
against her back and shoulders.

But he daren't. For not only would the fox certainly
bite him, but trusting one human might lead her to
trust others. And that meant going too close to guns
and snares—and cages!

Matt leaned back against the oak trunk and
breathed in the evening air, heavy with the scent of fox
and bluebells. But the usual peace and tranquillity of
the place evaded him because he was so angry and
worried. He felt rushed as well. He had been late setting off, and now he dare not linger in case he got into
trouble with his Dad. For a few moments Matt watched
the fox, who was busy with her supper. 'Bye, old girl,'
he said softly. 'See you tomorrow.'

Then, sadly, he made his way back home. As he
passed through the next-door garden, he glared at the
shouting figures outlined in the light from the cottage
window.

'By the end of the week, you'll be doing your
shouting somewhere else,' he promised.

Chewing-gum and Frogs

Cathy stood shivering at the bus-stop. It was a miserable day; the rain was bucketing down.

Matt stood as far away as he could without losing the scant comfort of the concrete shelter. He was smiling a little to himself.

Cathy took no notice of him at all as she wallowed in self-pity, her face huddled deep inside her coat. This was her first day at senior school. At her old school in Norwich, she would have had one more year of middle school before moving up. The transition was made slowly with day visits and joint school projects. Now she was being flung into this massive new school, a couple of weeks into term and with no help or warning. She did not even have the school uniform.

She was going to hate this, and she would make jolly sure her Mum knew just how awful the day had been—in exact detail. She was going to make her Mum feel really bad and guilty for making her go through with this!

At the school gates, Matt stepped off the bus first and, with his most concerned expression, civilly offered to take Cathy to reception. She could not refuse and had no choice but to follow his rough ginger mop past the thousands of staring faces, all looking at her. How she wished the earth could swallow her up!

But worse was to come—when she was at long last led into a classroom, she was ushered to a seat next to that awful carrot-headed boy again.

'This is Matt Carter,' said her form tutor. 'He lives next door to you, although you probably haven't met yet.'

How naïve can a teacher be? Cathy wondered.

'You'll look after Cathy for a few days, won't you?' Miss continued, without a glance at Cathy's face to see whether she approved of the idea or not.

'Oh yes, I'll do that all right,' Matt murmured under his breath, with soft menace.

Cathy stole a sideways look at him and scowled. She was too angry and numb to protest. She would just have to sit through everything that was to come.

Outwardly, Matt's behaviour was faultless. He made sure he escorted her everywhere and explained everything that was necessary. But he was only biding his time. He got his big chance at break. Cathy wandered off to have a good cry in the girls' loo, and he found her bag. The sandwich box was on top. What fun this was going to be! Carefully, he tripped over her bag so that the box fell out. Then, as it skidded across the floor, he picked it up and put it in his own bag. He was a good actor, and that was a piece of delicate timing and immaculate footwork. No one would have suspected that the complicated manoeuvre had been on purpose.

Next, he had to spread well-chewed gum across the finely grated cheese in Cathy's sandwiches. This was the difficult bit, but it worked. The box was returned to her bag with extreme deftness. Now all he had to do was wait...

Lunchtime was a triumph! Cathy gagged on her sandwiches as half the gum stuck to her teeth, and the other half was dragged down her throat by a crusty bit of bread. She was sick several times before returning to class. She looked pale and confused.

'Round 1!' Matt grinned, and shaved a nick in his pencil-box with a craft knife.

At home that evening, Cathy flew at her mother for putting 'foreign muck cheese' in her sandwiches, and went to bed straight away.

Matt crept slowly across the garden as usual, glancing up only briefly at the broken pane in the window that he guessed was probably Cathy's. But there was no pale face peering down at him. He was half relieved, and half insulted that she took so little interest in the fact that he was intruding upon her garden.

In truth, she was in a lonely heap, asleep in her damp-smelling bed.

The next day's 'lunch adjustments' had a certain element of poetic justice to it. Frogs from Cathy's own pond. Two small ones caught on the way home from feeding Vix. Excellent!

Cathy opened the box at lunchtime and just stared. The two frogs, damp, frightened and gulping air stared back at her. How golden and wondering their eyes were! Poor things, she thought. They're like me, scared and a long way from home.

'Someone fancies you!' one of the meaner girls from her form whispered loudly over Cathy's shoulder. 'Look everyone, our new Cathy's got a sweetheart, and he's sent her frogs to kiss and turn into a slimy thing just like him!'

Cathy glanced up at this and saw Matt scrambling up from the table with his cheeks flaming deep pink as only a carrot-head can do.

Aha, so it *was* him! Thanks for the tip-off, girls, she thought. Quietly she removed the frogs and took them outside to the ecology pond. They would be fine there. She found Matt had dumped her sandwiches in the bottom of her bag, so she sat alone in a corner and ate them while she thought.

As it happened, she liked frogs. In fact she liked all animals, except spiders of course. So Matt had not succeeded in achieving his aim of upsetting her, although he had made her angry. There must be some reason he wanted to scare her away; it must be more than the fact that she had stuck out her tongue at him on the first evening. Well, that wasn't so awful. Anybody would do that if someone was staring at them. But this was different. Things were developing into a challenge—and one that, despite herself, she was beginning to enjoy.

Next day she kept her bag well within sight and Matt did nothing. The following day was uneventful as well, so by the end of the week she had begun to relax her vigilance. Matt did not miss his opportunity, and successfully slipped something rather special into her PE bag.

When she tried to pull out her trainers and tugged

hard at what she thought was a wet shoelace, it came away in her hand. To her chagrin, Cathy screamed. Loudly. Then she dropped the bag. She had no idea what that awful, cold, muddy-squishy stuff all over her hands could be, but it was *revolting*! She tipped the contents of her PE bag on the floor and discovered several very squashed earthworms.

She pursed her lips tightly and scowled. 'Poor things!' she said. Then, as she dropped the still-wriggling worm-bits out of the window, she made a decision. 'This is *it*!' she promised herself. 'The time has come!'

It was a relatively easy job to lock Matt in the chemistry lab cupboard at the end of school. Matilda, the clever clogs who had suggested that Matt's frogs were a love token, was told that if she could get Matt to come back to the lab, then Cathy would make it worth her while. Matilda hinted to Matt that the headmaster was telling Cathy off and threatening to expel her. 'If you go into the lab cupboard, you'll hear it all through the wall of course,' she added with a gleeful grin. It was indeed true that many excellent conversations could be overheard from this point and Cathy suspected that this would be one her enemy just would not want to miss. She was right.

Matilda played her part perfectly, and Cathy parted with her week's pocket money without regret. Once Matt was inside, Cathy simply had to slam the door shut and lock it. He was a prisoner!

Happily she tossed the small key in her hand and wondered what to do next.

She didn't have to wait long. Matt rattled frantically at the door, then started to bang and scream.

'Let me out, for goodness sake!' he shouted. ' I can't stand being shut in! Please, help! Help!'

Cathy might have let him stew for a little longer, if it hadn't been for footsteps along the corridor...

The Wood 5 at Night

Cathy glanced back over her shoulder. It could be the caretaker, or it could be the Head...

She put her mouth to the lock of the cupboard door. 'I'll let you out if you shut up,' she whispered loudly.

Matt gasped and stopped his panic-stricken slapping of the door. 'Be quick, for crying out loud!'

The footsteps stopped, and adult voices could be heard just a little way off. Cathy spoke clearly through the keyhole again. 'First things first, I'll put the key in my pocket and walk away from here if you don't tell me why you're trying to upset me with frogs and things. You don't faze me at all. I *like* frogs, but you make me very angry because you're abusing animals. Secondly, I have no intention of being friends with you, so even when I do find out what's going on, I will never under any circumstances speak to you again. I just want to know what you're playing at.'

Just then the voices in the corridor moved on and the steps came nearer.

'I promise, but *please* let me out; I'll start scream-ing if you keep me in here. I'm not being silly, I'm claustrophobic. It's a real illness. *Please*, I really can't breathe...' Matt did sound desperate.

Cathy quietly turned the key and opened the door just as the science mistress came into the lab.

'Did you find them in there, Matt?' Cathy asked cheerfully. Then, turning to the teacher, she put on her brightest face. 'I lost my science notes, and Matt kindly offered to see if they'd been tidied up with the text-books,' she explained.

Matt came out, looking flushed. When the teacher thanked him for being so helpful to a new pupil and promised him a merit, he knew he could not start an argument then and there. 'Sorry, Cathy, your notes aren't in there,' he managed to mutter. 'Now, we'd better leg it, or we'll miss the bus back to Knapsden!'

The two ran as fast as they could to avoid further questions, and flung themselves onto the bus just as the doors were shutting. Cathy sat behind Matt and growled into his ear, 'Don't think you've got away with it; my vengeance can be *very* sweet indeed!'

Matt turned and met her glare with one equally venomous. 'I'll meet you by your garden pond at 8.30 pm tonight. Don't be late—unless you're scared of the dark, that is.'

***

Cathy was there on time. It wasn't quite dark. The first few stars were piercingly bright with the threat of a late frost. Cathy shoved her hands deep into her pockets and looked up into the sky. High above, in the purple darkness, seven or eight small, black shapes of bats darted to and fro, hunting for flying insects. For a fleeting moment, she was almost content. It was one of those magical evenings when one felt almost anything could happen—a time when other worlds—other possibilities were very close. She was so wrapped in her thoughts that she neither saw nor heard Matt as he slid through the shadows to her side.

What she did notice was the heavy smell of cheap dog food.

'Yuck!' she howled, 'What did you have for tea? Dogpoo stew?'

Matt did not reply, but his vague form beckoned her to follow. As they approached the barbed-wire fence, he took off his jacket and wrapped it around his hands. Then he pulled the wire high enough for Cathy to slide under without getting too muddy. He slithered after her and led the way up the chalky bank to the wood at the top. He moved swiftly, ducking and twisting between tree roots and low branches.

Cathy struggled to keep up but, not knowing the way, she stumbled over unseen tree roots and slipped as she trod bluebells underfoot and crushed their slimy stems. 'Why didn't you bring a torch, you moron? Or you could have warned me and I'd have brought one.'

'Shut up and keep quiet!' he warned, in a very firm but low voice. 'If you can't take it, go home. I'm just keeping my promise.'

Cathy said nothing, but felt the blood rising in her face and her throat tightening. She *would* get through this, and anything else he threw at her.

Suddenly, his dark form froze, his right hand outstretched to prevent her from moving forward. 'Ssshh!' he warned, 'Stay right here and don't move a muscle, or it'll all be ruined.'

Stealthily, he moved forward to the middle of a tangled hazel copse, its besom-like twigginess stark in the clear light of the rising moon. Cathy breathed slowly as the sense of magic and wonder met her again in the silhouetted contrasts of the night—black and umber branches weaving and entwining against the pale starlight in the indigo sky.

Occasionally, a rustle of tiny feet or the screech of a hunting owl broke the near silence of the night.

Matt had all but disappeared. If she had not watched carefully to see where his tall shape melted into the brushy trunks of the hazel copse, she would have lost him altogether. But she was determined that he would not give her the slip and leave her alone out here. From the high point where she stood, she could see the wood was not large. Fields stretched ahead and to her left and, by quietly turning around, she was sure she could see the lights of her own house, where she had left Mum sewing curtains. They had not come far, but getting back might be treacherous on her own.

She did not trust this ginger beanpole from next door. What was he up to?

Suddenly there was a short, harsh barking noise just ahead of her. She leaned forward slightly to see what was coming. Another similar bark answered the first, followed by a low shape like a small dog running (or was it limping?) towards Matt. The boy seemed to be bending over, and there was a tinny, scraping sound. Dog food! Of course, that awful smell! He kept a dog up here and was feeding it. But it must be a vicious one, Matt was not stroking it, or scratching its ears as he talked quietly to it.

Cathy held her breath. There was something wild

and thrilling about the scene that made her want to draw closer... She took one careful step. Suddenly, a twig snapped sharply under her foot, echoing in the cold clarity of the night like a gunshot.

The black animal shape shot away, and Matt stood up. Cathy could not see his face, but she could feel him glowering furiously at her.

He strode in her direction, grabbed her shoulder and shook it. 'Silly cow!' he growled. 'I told you to stay still. Now look what you've done! You've scared her away. I don't know whether she'll come back now. That's all she gets to eat, and she needs every scrap. I can't afford to give her more.'

Then he pushed roughly past her and ran all the way home.

Sliding down the bank he wriggled under the wire—without stopping to hold it up for her—and disappeared into the blackness between the trees. The blinding lights of their homes were shining vivid and yellow in the early night.

'Wait!' she gasped, as she ran across the garden after him. 'Wait! Matt... I'm sorry! Please stop and tell me about your dog.'

'It's not a dog—it's a fox, you moron!' snapped the disembodied voice out of the night. Then he was gone.

Cathy skulked about outside for a while, kicking angrily at the wall. Then she went inside.

***

Cathy could not get the idea of the wonderful half-tame fox out of her head all night. Next day at school, she tried every ruse she could to get Matt to talk to her, all without success. That evening, she was ready in the garden at 8.30 pm, watching every flicker or move-ment between the trees at the end.

Nothing happened, and it was almost nine when her mother opened the door and went out into the road, obviously watching for her.

'I'm here, Mum!' she called, just as a tall figure ran breathlessly past the gate, an empty dog food can in his hand.

Cathy followed her mother indoors without com-ment. But from next door, she could hear voices raised, and Matt's father yelled at him for being out too late.

Next day, she wrote him a note: 'Please talk to me—I'd like to help.' She stuck it firmly onto the handle of his bag while they were on the bus.

At break, he stopped her in the canteen. Standing firmly in her way, and peering down at her from his skinny height, red and irate. 'I don't want any help,' he said quietly, but firmly. 'I don't need you. Now, why don't you just shove off and leave me alone?'

Cathy was not going to be daunted. 'I can think of *far* worse things than chewing-gum in sandwiches. That's a primary school trick!' she jeered. 'Now either talk to me like a human being or risk my wrath for ever!' She was bluffing, but she knew that, with her long chestnut hair and dark eyes, she could glower very threateningly—and she played it to its best effect, frequently.

Matt looked out of the window in the direction of Knapsden with its precious wood. He wasn't at all scared of Cathy, but suddenly he did want to tell someone—and she knew half the story already. Perhaps he shouldn't have shown her Vix; he did not really know why he had done it. He just had. If he was going to tell anyone, it may as well be her.

He sighed. 'I'll tell you if you stop pulling silly faces at me and then leave me alone.'

'Sorry.' Cathy suddenly felt rather stupid.

Matt leaned on the window-sill with his face against the pane, just like he had when Cathy had first seen him. He looked as if he wished he could be in his wood with his beloved fox right now. Anywhere but here with *her*!

At first he said nothing, but then, hesitatingly, he began: 'Vix is about two years old. I found her in a poacher's snare last summer. The vet wanted to put her down—foxes can live with a damaged or missing back leg, but not a forepaw; they can't dig burrows or scratch in the earth for worms and stuff. I lied about my age to get a paper round so I can afford to feed her a tin of dog food every evening. She lives in empty badger burrows up on the knoll. Without me she'd die.

'She's all I've got in the world. Dad and me don't get on all that well, you see. Mum died when I was quite small, and he promised he'd always take good care of me—and he does. He spends all his time keeping everything sickeningly clean and making sure my homework is perfect—but he never just talks to me, or does anything with me just for fun. There's never any time—he's too busy trying to do everything right for Mum's sake. I feel terribly closed in all the time, and all this cleanliness really gets to me.

'For the past few years, while your cottage was empty, I used to escape into your garden. Then, I discovered an easy way into Foxdown Wood under the barbed wire. When I found Vix, it seemed the perfect

31

idea to put her there, where I could reach her easily to feed her.'

'But surely there're other ways into the wood?' Cathy felt things were beginning to fall into place at last. For the first time in ages someone was bothering to explain something properly to her. Matt's fox was important, and she found she wanted to help.

Matt shook his head. 'There is no other way into the wood—or at least it's virtually impossible. To the west, the farmer keeps all his other fences in such tight repair that it's impossible to get in, and to the east there are houses. I don't like going in other people's gardens... I don't make a habit of it. Yours was empty,' he added, defensively.

'The only other way in is via Longacre Lane. You might not know it—it's a track on the other side of the village. It's over half a mile round that way, then I've got to go through the wood and get to the knoll. There and back it's almost an hour's walk, including staying with Vix while she eats. I like to keep an eye on her—make sure she's all right and stuff. That's it, really,' he shrugged. 'Satisfied now?'

He got up to go.

Cathy caught hold of his sleeve. 'But why the chewing-gum and frogs?'

'Isn't that obvious?' Cathy could detect a bitter sob well hidden in his throat. 'I want you and your Mum to go away. I want my wild garden back, I want to be able to get to Vix easily. I have to do homework and study until 8.30 pm *every* night, and I have to be in the bath at 9 pm and in bed by 9.20 pm, with no exceptions. I just can't do it. I want my world back.'

Cathy felt a lump in her own throat. She knew how

that felt. But she wasn't ready to tell her tale—not to anyone. 'Can't you cycle round to Longacre Lane?'

'I haven't got a bike. Dad says they're dangerous. I do my paper round on foot.'

Cathy grabbed hold of his sleeve again, before he could even say he was going. 'Listen, there is something I can do to help. I can ask Mum if you can still cut through the garden. I've not been talking to her much lately, but she'd like your fox. She's OK like that.'

Matt stood up and shook his head violently. 'No! There must be no more people in Foxdown Wood. They might scare Vix off, and, and it's sort of... important up there, it's... *special* somehow. I can't explain why, it just is. There's something good up there, but I don't know what. If you told your Mum she'd be up there and goodness knows who else. And *you* mustn't go up again either, d'ye hear? It's *mine!*'

Then he turned and walked away, shoulders stiff, head held high, and saying nothing.

***

Next morning, Cathy was woken by a loud clattering at the door. It was only 6.45 am, and Matt, sodden from top to toe with driving rain, had already been standing on the doorstep for a good ten minutes, trying to make up his mind whether to knock or not.

He had so many conflicting thoughts in his head. Much as he resented the girl next door, she was the only one he could tell because she knew about Vix... He was bursting with anger and worry. Had to tell someone! Better tell her than someone at school. Cathy had seemed to care at least, whereas the kids in his class would just shrug. He didn't want anyone else to know about Vix anyway. Cathy knowing was more than enough. Now the worst seemed to be happening and he had to trust someone. But why did it have to be *her*? He wished she would go away. She was interfering and a nuisance. He was angry with himself for his need, but what else could he do?

In the end, he found himself knocking at Knighthayes Cottage. When Cathy opened the door and saw Matt cold and bedraggled on the doorstep, she beckoned him inside without question.

He was shaking as he held out a dripping copy of the local paper.

'Look... LOOK!' he begged. 'Look at this...'

Vix Makes a Decision

Cathy hastily introduced Matt to Mum as he peeled off his wet gear. He was too distracted to grunt more than a 'hello' as he spread a soggy newspaper across the kitchen table, making papier mâché mountains out of the marmalade and jam pots.

A small headline at the bottom of the front page announced 'Local Wood Sold'. Matt read the article aloud, while Maggie made large mugs of hot tea. 'But what's the fuss?' she queried. 'Developers buy up bits of land for housing everywhere. Things do change, you know. I'm not saying it's good, but it does happen, and like all changes we just have to live with it.'

Matt and Cathy swapped glances. 'Not *all* changes, Mum,' Cathy said meaningfully. 'Some things have to be fought.' Matt did not miss the bitter edge to her voice.

Mum looked from Matt to Cathy. 'Well, OK, you have a point. But are you going to tell me why I've been woken at this unearthly hour to meet the next-door neighbour and to be told about a proposed plan to build some new houses?'

Matt shook his head warningly, and Cathy said nothing. Matt swallowed his tea, scalding his throat, and folded the newspaper. 'No, sorry, Mrs... ?'

'Maggie. I'm not a Mrs any more, and you're old enough to call me by my first name. Maggie will do just fine.'

'Sorry to have woken you, Maggie. I was just a bit upset, that's all. I forgot how early it was.' And with that he grabbed at his newspaper satchel and water-proofs and ran out of the door.

'Well! Do you know what that was about?'

Cathy was, unusually for her, busying herself with cutting her own sandwiches. 'Another pot of tea, Mum?' She had to play it cool. Foxdown Wood's magic was becoming important to her as well. She felt secretly thrilled that Matt had entrusted her with his need to save the wood. Not that she wanted to be friends, of course, but she felt a sort of triumph. How could she explain it all, anyway? Mum hadn't seen her point over leaving Norwich. How would she explain about Vix and the special feeling the wood gave her? Mum never seemed to understand anything.

Maggie said nothing, but accepted the fresh tea and went to light the sitting-room fire.

After school, Matt came round again and together they poured over the 'planning permission' section of the newspaper. 'Fifty new executive homes! You'll have to find somewhere else for Vix to go!'

'I can't,' said Matt, miserably, 'not near enough for me to be able to feed her.'

'Perhaps she could go to one of those sanctuary places? She'd be looked after there.'

Matt pulled his fine red brows down and made a face. He felt very angry. 'You don't understand, do you? I should have known better than to tell you all this. How would you like to be a wild animal suddenly dumped in a pen? Even if it was a huge pen, she'd die of grief at being shut in. I know I would,' he added wistfully, glancing out at the rain-drenched garden. But it's not just Vix, there are barn owls and tawnies and some really unusual fungi growing there. It'll upset the balance of *everything* if the wood goes. But more than that, it's the place itself, it's...'

'Special, I know,' Cathy finished off his sentence for him. 'You're going to think me daft, Matt,' she added, but I think we ought to go and tell Vix. It's her wood, after all.'

Matt stared at Cathy hard. He wanted to say, 'What a stupid idea,' because it didn't make any sense, and he didn't like her anyway. But instead he picked up his coat and said, 'I'll do my homework now, and see if I can get off early. Vix will still be asleep at the moment.'

***

Matt's knock at the door just before sunset made Cathy jump. 'I'm off, Mum,' she called, as she pulled on her jacket.

'Where, dear?'

'I'm going for a walk with Matt. A bit of fresh air before bed and all that.'

Maggie shook her head as Cathy shot out into the night. Something was going on, but she did not know what. She wished so much that Cathy would realize that she wasn't against her. Some things were just unavoidable—and some things were, well, just the best that circumstances would allow. Still, if she was off for a walk with the lad from next door, perhaps Cathy was settling in a bit, after all.

The woods were still damp and slippery, although the morning's torrential rain had drained away into the chalky soil fairly well. The smell of wet spring soil had so much life in it that it made Cathy feel exhilarated. She ran after Matt agilely, as if she knew every root and stump as well as he did. The glorious haze of blue and mauve bells underfoot contrasted with the canopy of fresh, green leaves above. The evening was so invigorating, it seemed impossible that any evil fate could hang over such a perfect place as Foxdown Wood. Cathy and Matt moved quickly towards the knoll, forgetting for the moment that they were supposed to be at odds with each other.

When they reached the knoll, Vix was already there, looking over the fields beyond. Cathy waited a few strides away, while Matt scraped the tin of dog food out onto the ground. Then he knelt down and spoke quietly to the small fox while she ate her meal.

When she had finished, instead of running away into the night as usual, the vixen sat back and looked at Matt—Boy as she called him. There was urgency— even fear—in his eyes. Then she glanced towards the other one, the female human hidden in the shadows. To Vix, Cathy looked and smelled anxious. How she wished she could understand human words! But she *could* understand their feelings. Vix knew that Boy and his friend were trying to tell her something vital. *Now* was the time to trust him! Now was the time to take him to the Other World, where she sensed they would understand each other perfectly.

Something told her that Methwin needed to know about this, whatever it was. What Boy was trying to say might be what the King was searching for so desperately. This was important enough for them all to risk the dangers of the Other World.

She sniffed the air. There was no scent of danger, not like when the strange male humans came thumping around the wood in heavy boots and dropping stinking little hot things that burned her paw. No, it felt safe. She would risk it. She dared not stop to worry about it.

Vix stood and limped a few paces. Then she turned and looked back at Boy and the other human. She gave one of her funny barks, then walked a little further on.

'What's the matter Vix?' Matt asked softly. 'Does your paw hurt?' He took a step towards her, pulled off his jacket and wrapped it over his hand to protect against her inevitable bite while he examined her. But she avoided him and ran a little further away, and barked again.

'Do you think she wants us to follow her?' Cathy asked.

'I suppose there could be an injured animal ahead or something.'

'Perhaps she's had cubs,' Cathy suggested.

'No, I'd know if she'd had cubs. There's not been a dog fox up here, oh, not for ages. If she had a partner he'd still be around; they're very faithful.'

'Unlike humans,' Cathy added, ruefully.

'I guess so.' Matt wasn't really listening, but Vix was off again. 'Look, there she goes, between those old tree roots!'

'My, they're huge!' Cathy whistled, admiring the huge, massy shapes that suddenly rose up around her in the dark. They seemed so sad, so demolished. Uprooted and thrown aside. Cathy felt for them.

Matt spoke, interrupting Cathy's thoughts. 'Last winter's storms blew a lot of trees over, especially the big ones. These were wonderful oaks once, now there's just a huge chalky hollow left. Look, see where Vix is going, the roots form a sort of tunnel there...'

The two slid on loose chalk and flints as they slithered down into the dip after the small vixen. Her lithe, dark shape stood out strongly in the last rays of spring sunlight, as she slipped down the narrow tunnel Matt had been talking about.

'This should lead to...' Matt's voice trailed away.

Suddenly, Cathy slipped and slid into Matt's back, pushing him forward so he stumbled out of the damp, English evening, through the tunnel into... broad summer daylight!

Methwin

'Hurry up, it's not safe here!'

Matt and Cathy looked around to see who was speaking. Only Vix was nearby, looking up at them with an anxious face.

'Who said that?' Matt looked confused.

'I did. Please hurry. You can ask the King your questions. He understands things. We don't have time now!'

There was no doubt about it—it was Vix herself! Cathy had seen her mouth move. Or had she? 'Matt, is this a trick? Are you doing ventriloquism?' she asked, nervously.

'Oh, please hurry!' Vix begged, looking worriedly over her shoulder at the humans.

Yet there seemed to be nothing to be frightened of—except that they were suddenly in a different place... or was it? Behind them was the beech and hazel wood they had just left. Yet it was not quite the same, although Matt couldn't have explained how it was different. Ahead and on both sides was a wide, open chalk down landscape, which seemed to be empty, apart from a few clusters of trees and woods cloaking the surrounding hillsides.

Vix gave a short bark and began to run ahead, then stopped and turned back. Then she did the same again in a very agitated manner.

Matt and Cathy exchanged glances. Animals did not talk, but the anxiety in Vix's behaviour was all too plain to see. Without any more argument, they followed her down the slope that would have led towards Longacre Lane if they had been in Knapsden. Then they turned to the left, which should have been ploughed fields, but instead was a continued wide expanse of open chalky landscape. Further to their left, nestled in a hollow not far from the edge of the wood, was a small settlement of circular wooden houses with a long, thatched, wooden hall in their midst.

In this Other World, it was a warm, midsummer's day, with the air full of the scent of wild blue chicory and the tough springy grass alive with minute chalk-hill blue butterflies. High above, a pair of red kites circled lazily on a thermal, watching for small prey on the ground. How could somewhere so peaceful be a dangerous place?

'Isn't it lovely?' Cathy panted, as she trotted behind Matt and the fox.

'It won't be if we don't hurry!' Vix replied. 'Now *please* stop looking at the view and run—they're coming, I can smell them!'

Matt and Cathy could not ask 'who' was coming, as the fox was well ahead.

As they left the shelter of the wood's edge and came towards the settlement, they saw that the scattered buildings were surrounded by a tall palisade of pointed stakes. The gateway they were approaching had a square wooden tower built on either side of it, with lookouts posted on each one.

As the fox approached, she barked: 'They're coming! Let us in—these are my friends!'

The gates swung open to admit them and they scrambled down a steep chalky bank. Suddenly, Matt stopped dead and gasped, 'But that's just about where our houses should be, Cath, look!'

'Almost, but not quite,' Cathy was about to say, when suddenly a whistling sound and a stinging breath of air caught her ear. Vix was well ahead, running through the gateway. Cathy turned round to see a band of tall men and women in white, large-sleeved shirts and short, brightly-coloured jackets, running very fast towards them. One had a fresh arrow firmly placed in his bow. And he was already pulling the string...

Cathy squealed frantically, and ran very fast after Vix and Matt, flinging herself to safety.

Once inside the wooden palisade, the heavy log gates were firmly slammed behind them and barred into place. Cathy and Matt collapsed on the ground, hardly able to breathe.

'Come inside,' boomed a deep voice from above their heads. 'If you are friends of the brave fox, you are welcome indeed.'

The children looked up... and up... and up. Peering down at them from a very lofty height was an immensely tall, dark-eyed man with a long, white, plaited beard and a wide, leaf-green robe.

Vix came and sniffed at Matt. 'This one is Boy—I've told you about him before, My Lord, and this is a young female. I don't know her. She came with Boy. I think he trusts her.'

The tall man knelt down, so he could see his visitors more clearly. His eyes were kind, but he had the look of a teacher who would never suffer late homework.

Matt looked at him, then at Cathy. 'Yes,' he said, then unexpectedly he added, 'I trust her, she's my friend.'

'Then come inside,' boomed the huge man, who must have been nearly two metres high at least. 'I am King Methwin. Welcome to my lodge. It is called Knight Hayes.'

Matt and Cathy looked at each other in amazement, but neither had a chance to speak as tall, handsome people were helping them to their feet and ushering them into the hall. Inside, the lodge was light and surprisingly airy, with large windows at each end. The walls were draped with colourful tapestries that swayed gently in the summer air. The king turned to his guests and gestured to them to sit.

'How may I call you? I expect Boy and Female are not your real names. Then tell me what your business is in my land, for I can see you are not of my people. I have met others like you, but not for a very long time,' he added, rather sadly.

After the introductions had been made and everyone was seated and provided with oatcakes and fruit juice, Matt seemed stumped for words. Cathy, who always had something to say for herself, began: 'As to what we are doing here, well, Sir, I don't really know. We sort of fell into your world, following Vix.'

At this, Vix joined in. 'As you know, My Lord, in my world, Boy looks after me and feeds me. Tonight, something was troubling him, something deep, causing him great pain. But I could not understand his words, so I led him and Cathy here, where all words are clear, so I would be able to understand him. Forgive me if I have led danger to your door. Please do not be angry, My Lord,' she added timidly, 'I felt it was urgent... I hoped it might be the news that you have been so anxious to know.'

The King smiled and stroked the fox's rich, russet-brown head. 'No, I'm not angry, little fox. Thank you for doing your best.' Then he turned to Matt and Cathy. 'Tell us, young ones,' his deep voice boomed, 'what is your urgent message for the fox?'

Matt looked at Vix, and then at the King. Now he understood part of why Foxdown Wood always seemed so important to him; he had sensed it really was a place where strange things might happen. Perhaps his message *would* be important here too, though he could not explain why. He pulled out the tattered newspaper clipping from his pocket and passed it to the King.

Methwin took it, looked at it the right way up, and then upside down. 'I am sorry, my boy—I cannot read your signs!'

Matt was obviously shocked: a king who could not read? His amazement must have shown on his face, because the King laughed. 'I can read well enough, but not *your* signs. We are not speaking your words, but we are listening with the heart. Lies are always known here, for they show, like a boil on the nose. Now, in your own way, tell me your news.'

The King and Vix listened attentively while Matt explained about the wood and what planning permission meant, and Cathy described what a housing estate was. The whole process took a little time, but at last Methwin nodded gravely. He was not a young man, but he looked wise. He nodded as he listened, and stroked his tightly-plaited, silvery beard. He looked very sad and not a little worried.

'I think I understand,' he said at last.

Vix looked up and gave a sharp bark. 'My Lord, could it be that your troubles are seeping through into our world?'

'I fear so, my friend.' The King stroked her rich, red fur again. 'You see, our worlds, as I think you both already understand, are closely interwoven. We are in different dimensions but in the same place. We are, if you like, coexisting.'

'At the same time?' Cathy asked, amazed.

'*Time* is a strange word, my dear,' the King smiled. 'Yes, we do coexist, and yet we don't, and not "at the same time" as you put it. It is very difficult, and I am not at all sure I understand it. I have never been to your reality, and few have ever come here. But what happens in your world is inextricably connected to events in ours. Our land is under threat, and we wondered if yours was as well. That is usually the way between our two worlds. They seem to be held in balance, with the wood at the centre of both.

'This brave fox has been keeping me informed of the comings and goings in your world, but I could not make head or tail of much of it. Short men with little hot sticks and grey clothes, walking around with strange machines? It is all beyond our ken. The fox cannot understand many of your words, so we could put no meaning on anything.

'But your story of the danger to the wood makes much sense. The wood is the centre of my Kingdom. Although I have many great and rich cities, wide farms and fish-filled lakes, I come to this little place here when I need to be quiet, or to think. The wood is an ancient meeting place for people to come and talk with the Guardian of my land. I do not always understand his words, but I find being here gives me much wisdom and peace of mind.

'I came here some weeks ago because I am troubled by my nephew, Harawed. He wants to take my place as King. It was his warriors who chased you here. He found out I was coming to this lodge by the wood and now he has me surrounded. I cannot get back to my city, and I cannot send for help. I must just wait to see what happens.'

'That's terrible!' Matt gasped. 'Could we get a message through for you?'

The king smiled and shook his head. 'My captains do not know you. They may not trust your word. They would not trust even Vix, for foxes are unknown in our land. Besides, the problem is not one that can be solved by battles and warfare. But I do not know what the solution is. The Guardian has called me and Harawed to this place, for it is here where Kings and Queens come to be made... and to end their reigns...' he added, sadly. 'Whatever happens must be faced with the few friends and warriors I have with me.'

'But surely we could at least put up a good fight?' Cathy leaned forward in her chair, glowing with enthusiasm. 'You are the King, after all!'

Methwin shook his head. She reminded him so much of his daughter, of so long ago...

'I am not worried about holding on to my throne. My days of being a good leader are numbered. I am happy to step down, but not to make room for him. He would treat people like slaves and misuse them. There would be no hope or freedom left in the land. I had intended, with the help of the Guardian, to give my Kingship to my people. It is time they ruled themselves.

'But legend says that in times gone past, people came from your world bearing words of great strength. Some say it was "magic", but I think it was deeper, more powerful than that. It was something of the Guardian's doing.'

'But does this Guardian live in your world or ours? Can we go and get him for you?' Cathy volunteered. 'We must be able to do *something* to help?'

Methwin looked up at the sunlight playing on the beams of the great hall. 'I thank you, child. But the Guardian of the Wood lives neither here nor there, and you cannot "get" him for me. He is here already, or you would not have come. Only those he summons can cross between the two worlds. The fact that you are here shows that ancient ways are stirring again... Or else the walls between the Worlds are thinning and failing...' he added sadly, under his breath.

The King stopped stroking Vix and stood. He looked huge and immovable, like a great chestnut tree. 'My hope is that the words of strength that were uttered in the old days may be spoken here again, and that the Guardian will protect my people from this tyrant.'

He began to pace up and down the hall, his wide, leaf-green robe flowing out behind him like a great sea in the summer breeze.

'Many people say the Guardian is an ancient myth and the wood is merely haunted. Be that as it may, I am in no doubt, we must both win in our own Worlds, or things will never be at peace again in either place.'

Just then, much shouting was heard at the gate. 'We're under attack!' someone yelled. The King shrugged his fine, green robe onto a chair and then, clad in leather and chain mail like any ordinary soldier, he strode towards the door and took a long, lethal sword from the rack that hung there.

He turned and hesitated. 'I am tired of fighting. It is not the solution to anything,' he said. 'But if you can discover how to find those who bring words of great strength, that would be a great service, and one that I believe will benefit your world as well. The Guardian must have summoned you here, or else you would not have passed through the narrow space between our worlds. There is a purpose to your coming.'

'But we've *got* to fight!' Cathy started to say. 'I'm not scared, I'll help!'

But Matt put a quiet hand on her arm. 'We'll see what we can find out and come back tomorrow, straight after school,' he promised.

'Quick,' Vix hissed. 'There is a small gate at the back which leads to the wood. These men prefer to fight in the open, as they are so tall and their swords are so long. We will be safe if we are swift and quiet.'

The three of them slipped through the small gateway and dashed as fast as they could up the bank and towards the shelter of the trees.

Cathy's lungs were burning by the time they were safe amongst the trees. Catching her breath for a moment, she glanced back at the twenty or so tall warriors, some fair, some dark, but all with thick, bushy hair tied back with red kerchiefs and white billowing shirts under their mail. They looked like an illustration from a picture-book. It wasn't real. It couldn't be.

Suddenly she realized that Matt and Vix had both dived into the tunnel between the tree roots, and everything went black as she too plunged back into the night of the everyday world.

It was raining again.

Many Plans

Matt looked at his watch as they came into the light from Cathy's sitting-room window. 'Crumbs! It's just coming up to 8.45 pm. We must have been in the Other World for about three-quarters of an hour.'

'We'll have to keep an eye on the time if we ever go there again,' Cathy added, 'You know what your Dad is like if you're late.'

'I don't need reminding,' Matt replied ruefully. 'And talking of that, I'd better fly.'

Cathy called after him, 'We *did* go somewhere, didn't we... I mean, it was real, wasn't it? Or did we sort of make it up somehow?'

Matt shrugged. 'I don't know how we can tell, but *you* think we did, don't you?'

'Yes, but I sort of dream lots of things...' Cathy hesitated. 'And, whether its real or not, I want to try to help King Methwin and his people. I'd like to do something there to help, but I don't know what it might be. Whoever used to come "with words of strength" must surely be dead by now. But we might be able to find some more good words.' Then she hesitated and bit her lip. 'Do you think that's stupid to try to help someone who might not be real?'

Matt shrugged, 'I want to help save Foxdown Wood, and that's very real. If chasing a fantasy is the only way to do it—well, it doesn't *feel* such a stupid idea, even if it doesn't make any logical sense. That place may or may not be real, but my Dad is, and so is our clock. I must go, we'll talk about it tomorrow.'

***

Cathy sat in bed until very late, making lists of 'words of strength' to take to the Other World. She started with 'Supercalifragelisticexpialidocious', 'Hey presto!', 'Open sesame!' and 'Abracadabra', and 'then she tried to think of *sensible* words... like, like what? Suddenly she tore the paper up. It was daft! It was silly, it was just a game, an elaborate shared dream she and Matt had been having.

Then there were problems with her Mum. Cathy had come in on the stroke of 9 pm just as she had promised, but as soon as she walked through the door she was met with endless questions of 'Where've-you-been? Who've-you-been-with?' It was bad enough being holed up in the back of nowhere with too much Mum and no Dad, but as soon as it looked as if she was making her own friends and doing her own thing, it was like the Spanish Inquisition. So she had flounced off to bed, ignoring conciliatory offers of hot milk and biscuits.

***

The next day, Cathy did not see much of Matt, as they were in different groups for most subjects. But on the way home from school Matt shoved a note into her pocket while they stood at the bus-stop (they never sat next to each other on the bus, that would have been just *too* embarrassing).

'Communication!' was all the note said. Cathy scratched her nose. Had Matt flipped? What on earth was he on about?

'What do you mean "communication"?' Cathy demanded, as soon as they were off the bus.

'Communication *is* "words of strength"... don't you see? Words are nothing, they are just useless sounds, unless they're heard... unless they *mean* something. So let's take some means of communication to King Methwin. Then he can send messages to his captains to come and rescue him! It's simple!' Matt announced, triumphantly.

'But I thought he said that fighting wasn't the answer...?' Cathy said, cautiously. *She* was the one who had advocated making a good fight, and had been firmly told she was wrong—or so she had felt.

'I said "rescue"—not "fight"!' Matt grinned. He gave her a playful punch in the arm. 'You'll see! Communication is what makes words "strong". It's *got* to be the answer!...'

Cathy was not sure, but could not think of any real objection. Neither could she think of any better idea, so she shrugged. Matt was on a roller-coaster of excitement. 'OK,' she said, 'so what do we do now?'

'That's the best bit!' he laughed, 'We have the whole weekend ahead, and for once I have absolutely no homework tonight. Even Dad can't make me do what isn't there!' He tossed his bag high in the air, and grimaced as it came down with a horrific crash on the pavement. 'Oops!' he winced. 'I forgot I'd got a jam jar in there, it was Home Ec. today. I'll meet you in your garden in half an hour.'

It was only after he disappeared inside that she realized that she didn't have the foggiest idea what he'd been talking about: what *sort* of communication? She shrugged. She'd just have to wait and see.

Cathy's Mum wasn't in when she opened the door. A note propped up by the kettle told her where the cakes were, and 'Back ASAP. Unexpected events!'

Cathy changed into her jeans, grabbed several cakes, added 'me too' at the end of Mum's note, and ran into the garden.

Matt was already there, clutching two small, black, oblong boxes triumphantly. 'Walkie-talkies!' he grinned, they're really good ones, they've got a four kilometre range. They cost a fortune. I had them for my last birthday, but I've never really used them. No one to use them with, if you see what I mean. Now let's run—Dad isn't home from work yet, so if I slip the leash now, I should have a couple of hours free. Good, eh?'

Hardly had the two reached the end of the garden when the phone rang in Matt's house.

'I'll have to answer it, Cathy. If it's Dad he'll blow his top if I'm not here, as he thinks I ought to be.'

He returned a few minutes later looking utterly miserable. 'Dad wants me to do a load of shopping, and, would you believe it, *wash the skirting-boards* in the living-room!'

Cathy stood with her mouth open, 'Wash the skirting-boards!' she repeated incredulously. 'Does *anybody* wash skirting-boards?'

'Dad does,' Matt moaned, kicking a stone hard with

his trainer. He looked up and shrugged. 'I'll have to go, I've got such a lot to do. If I don't do it I'll be grounded, but if do it well, I might even get an extension.'

'What's an extension?'

'It means I can stay out late. Then we could have a really good long time in Methwin's world!'

'If it really exists,' Cathy added miserably, chomping on a cake. 'Here. Have one of these to cheer you up. Let me know when you're free.'

Matt looked up at the wood thoughtfully. 'Even if it doesn't exist, it's still sort of fun wishing it did. It makes everything here a bit less drab and humdrum, don't you think?'

'Sort of escaping from it all?'

'Maybe. Not quite. Better than that.' He waved crumby fingers up at the bedroom windows. 'Which room is yours?'

'The one with the broken window. It's freezing,' Cathy added with feeling.

'Thought so. Mine's the other side of the wall.'

'I know, I saw you there, the first day.' Then she blushed, wishing she hadn't stuck out her tongue *quite* so rudely.

Matt remembered too. He stuck his tongue out and grinned. 'See you later. I'll knock on my bedroom wall when I'm ready. This might have to be a sneak-out job.'

Cathy was amazed that Matt could take such rotten luck with such good humour—but then, he did have something to look forward to. And maybe the idea of a sneak-out appealed to her as well.

Matt had already disappeared down the road with the shopping bag when it occurred to her that maybe she could have taken the walkie-talkies to the King.

However, it was Matt's fox and his world, so perhaps it wouldn't be fair. But there was nothing to stop her going to see the king and telling him help was on the way.

Cathy felt a swell of excitement. Of course! At least that was something she could do!

The path to the knoll and the fallen trunks beyond was beginning to feel very familiar to Cathy and she was sure that if necessary, she could do the walk in the dark on her own. As she approached the chalky tree-root tunnel, she stopped and peered nervously into the hollow.

It seemed a very strange and discomforting thing to do—to slide from one world into another. It suddenly occurred to her, was it safe?

Suddenly she heard voices. A little way ahead, just the other side of the hazel copse, two men were talking. Between them they had several sheets of plans and a theodolite.

Their faces were turned away, but one had grey hair and was a little stooped. They were both dressed in grey business suits and looked very respectable. But what they were saying belied their looks in every way. Cathy sank down into the hollow. She did not like the *feel* of these men at all.

'We'll flatten this knoll and use the flints and topsoil to fill in the dew pond on the other side, then the main centre of the development will be to our left, over there,' the older man pointed towards Longacre Lane.

'Have we sorted out the planning department yet?' asked the second man.

'Easy, they swallowed all the yarns I spun, like a baby swallowing chocolate drops! It's amazing what real-looking documentation you can make with a decent PC these days.'

The second man laughed. I've got sales of 75 per cent of the properties in the bag with a local estate agent, who thinks he's buying a real bargain. The rest are almost sewn-up. One of the local firms looks as if it'll buy them for cheap housing, to attract new employees. The fact that everything will fall down within a few years will be neither here nor there. We'll be sunning ourselves somewhere hot with no extradition agreement. The houses will be rubble, and no one will be able to touch us.'

The first man folded up his plans. 'I hope the bull-dozers can move in by the end of next week, as soon as the sale's completed. Everything should be signed and sealed at the Council's Housing Committee meeting tomorrow afternoon, if there're no protests from local residents. I made sure the date for close of objections was wrong, so people will think they've got ages instead of twenty-four hours!'

'Brilliant!' laughed the younger man. 'Have you done? We ought to get going now.'

The older man looked around. 'Yes, I think so.'

Suddenly, Cathy sneezed, so unexpectedly, she had scarcely felt it coming.

'Hey, what's that?' both men turned at the sound. With a few bounds the younger man was standing at the top of the dip where Cathy was hiding under a huge chalk-clogged tree root. Kicking hard she tried to wriggle backwards into the Other World, but she could not find the way in. Her feet just met hard earth and chalk, however much she kicked and prodded with her feet. She felt cold creeping up and down her spine, as she realized with horror... There *was* no Methwin's Land!

In sheer panic, she flattened herself as hard as she could into the ground, certain there was no escape. As she did so, there was a harsh barking noise and an angry snarling just above her head.

The younger man laughed. 'It's just a fox! A vixen, by the look of her. We must have strayed near her cubs. The bulldozers will see to them. I might bring my gun and have some fun at the same time.'

'It didn't sound like a fox,' said the older man, warily.

'What else could it have been?'

Just then, Vix took a step forward and bared her sharp little teeth threateningly.

'Looks like she's injured. An angry vixen can rip a man's arm open if there are cubs around, and an injured animal is even worse,' said the younger man nervously. 'Come on, Dad,' he urged. 'We've done everything we need to here. It's starting to rain. Let's get back.'

The older man looked back suspiciously at the hollow where Cathy was hiding. Then, he turned up his collar against the rain which was beginning to fall hard. 'I guess so,' he said, and followed his son down the back towards the lane.

Cathy waited for the sound of a car engine before breathing deeply and wriggling out of her hiding-place. 'Thanks Vix!' she said, but the young fox only stared at her, terrified, and scurried away as fast as her lame forepaw would allow.

Sneak-out

Cathy felt miserable as she walked home in the rain. The afternoon was chilly and wet, but what made her feel really low was that the Other World did not exist.

Somehow the thought of something special, something different and exciting just for her—or at least somewhere that didn't involve unreliable grown-ups—had made her feel good for the first time in a long while. She'd known it was daft to think that it might really have existed, but somehow the thought that it didn't was devastating.

She would have to break the news to Matt. Going to the Other World had been a good game while it lasted, and not everything was lost. There was still Vix to feed in the evenings, if Matt would let her go with him. But inside she was still very cross. Yet another bit of her life that she cared about had been snatched away from her. She was cross, too, for having let herself believe in anything quite so half-baked.

Nothing in life could be trusted—*nothing!*

She grunted at her Mum as she walked through the

kitchen, flung her coat in a damp heap in the corner and went upstairs to wash and put dry clothes on. She listened very hard for any sounds of knocking on the bedroom wall upstairs, but there was nothing. After tea, she grudgingly helped her Mum wash up, then muttered something about going upstairs to read. She did not feel well at all. It wasn't just the sulks, she was feeling hot and shivery.

Maggie offered a hot-water bottle, and was rewarded with an indecipherable moan, so she just shrugged and looked sad as Cathy disappeared upstairs.

Cathy was woken several hours later by a scratching sound. It was quite dark. The noise was getting louder—and louder—until suddenly there was a crash and a thump, and a dusty-smelling shadow landed heavily on the end of her bed.

'Don't scream!' Matt hissed. 'It's only me!'

Cathy sat up. 'I thought I was dreaming,' she said sleepily. 'How did you get in, anyway?'

'Through the attic. I often come this way if I'm grounded or something. It's the only way out once Dad has bolted the door downstairs. Our stairs creak as well and I'd never get out without being caught.' He shone his torch up at the ceiling. A huge black rectangle gaped above them both. Then he shone the torch on his own face. He was grinning insanely and looked really spooky. 'Are you ready?'

'For what?' Cathy was groping with reality. She felt really hot and ill, and could not remember what she was supposed to be doing at all.

Matt shone the torch on her. 'What's the matter?'

'Don't feel well.'

'Too ill to come to see Methwin?'

'Too ill to live, I think,' she groaned as she pulled the covers up under her chin again.

'Oh well,' Matt whispered, 'I'll go alone. You do look pretty awful, I must say. I'm afraid I'll have to disturb you again tonight. This is the only way in, once Dad has bolted the door downstairs, but I'll be as quiet as I can. I'll use a chair to get back up, rather than bouncing on your bed, like I used to do before you came...'

And with that he swung himself out of the window, perched on the outhouse roof below, then half slithered, half jumped down to the ground.

There was a terrific clatter and 'OUCH! That dustbin never used to be there!' And he was gone.

'He could have shut the window after him,' Cathy muttered as she got out of bed to do it. As she settled down to sleep again, she tossed and turned anxiously. There was something vital she had to tell him, something about the Other World. But her head ached so much she could not remember.

***

Next day, Cathy just slept. Once or twice she vaguely wondered how Matt had got on and what time he had come in. He must have done it very quietly; she had not heard him clambering up the slates, or climbing past her to get back into the attic. Perhaps he had a key to his own house and had gone back through the door like most people. He had said something about not being able to get in any other way, but she couldn't remember why. All this clambering was very silly really.

After lunch, she began to feel better, and tried a few tentative knocks on the wall between their rooms.

No answer. She climbed on a chair and put the hatch down over the attic entrance. There was a terrible draught from the hole. She felt cross he hadn't bothered to shut it.

There was a draught coming from the broken window as well. She chuckled as she realized the hole in the glass wasn't an accidental break—it had been carefully made, so someone outside could insert a hand through the pane to open the window catch. Matt said this was his usual route. He must have done it! Then she looked at it again. The catch handle was left pulled tightly down, just as she had left it the night before. How odd.

But she took no further notice.

Just before tea, she thought she heard noises coming from Matt's room, so she knocked on the wall again. The shuffling sound continued, but with no answering knock.

Cathy came down for tea, but stared absently out of the window the whole time. Where was Matt? What time would he be going to feed Vix? What had happened last night? Oh crumbs! Now she remembered what she had to tell Matt—that the Other World wasn't real!

She laughed a little to herself and stared down at her mug of tea. He'd have found out the truth fairly quickly and come home all muddy. That was why he hadn't come back through the window. He'd been filthy.

Maggie pushed some chocolate eclairs across the table. 'Share the joke, love?'

Cathy had forgotten all about her mother's existence. She looked up quite surprised. 'No. Sorry, just something at school that made me chuckle. Nothing really.'

Maggie had felt quite lonely for the last few days. Cathy had been out so much and when she was home she was asleep. It made her sad because she had tried so hard to make their new home comfy and a nice place for them to be together.

'Guess where I went yesterday?' she chirped enthusiastically. 'You know I was out when you came home from school?'

Cathy shrugged. She vaguely remembered, but she had other things on her mind. 'Oh?'

Maggie got up from the table, grinning. She put out her hand and caught Cathy's fingers, tugging at her playfully. She was almost bouncing with excitement. 'Come and see, love! I've got a surprise! I've bought a second-hand telly and... wait for it, a video player! And, to top the lot, I've hired out a James Bond movie— what d'you think?'

But Maggie's triumph was cut short. Cathy tugged away her hand, ran to the back door and opened it.

There was a voice calling urgently in the dark of the wood to their right: 'Matt, Matthew, where are you?'

Claustrophobia!

Matt was a long way from being able to hear his Dad.

He was lying very cold and stiff, hardly able to move, and facing his greatest terror—claustrophobia!

Gingerly, he moved his head. It throbbed and ached unbearably.

Everything was so dark and cold... and hard! He shifted his body. Every muscle burned, and something was digging into his back.

Why was his bed so noisy? His head spun, he felt very sick and confused. Now he realized he was not in bed, but where else could he be? He laid his cheek down where a pillow should have been. Everything was cold and hard and gritty.

He tried to wipe the tiny stones away with his hand, but his arms did not respond. His wrists hurt.

Slowly it dawned on him that he was lying, tied up, on a concrete floor somewhere a long way from anywhere, quite alone.

And, what was worse, he was shut in. Slowly, steadily, the idea pulsed and swelled, pressing in on him like a living nightmare. Closed in! *CLOSED IN!* No way out!

Closed in. Shut up. No door. Locked. Thrown away the key. Forgotten... The thoughts chanted inside his head, again and again. Pressing in on him, until the words began to feel physical and heavy... then even heavier, like stones or lead piled on his chest, making it hard to breathe... He could feel his chest working for air, he had to breathe, he could not let these feelings win. His eyes stung, as tears welled up under the lids. He would not give in to his fear. He must not panic.

'There is air, all around you,' he told himself out loud. 'This is not a stuffy place. You are not shut in a cupboard. So calm down and think!' he commanded. 'Where are you? Where *were* you? What are you doing here—wherever this is?'

He laid his head down again and breathed, steadily and deeply, trying to control his racing heartbeat and the feeling of terror that was threatening to overwhelm him. 'Breathe one, two, three, four, five, and blow gently out...' he tried his relaxation exercises. He tried again, but his voice cracked into fear at 'three' and he found himself screaming, no words, nothing intelligent like 'help', just terrified screaming from the lower throat.

Suddenly his self-control snapped. Frantically, he rocked and thrashed and kicked, his screams becoming howls of anguish, as he bayed like a snared creature, alone and unheard.

After a while, his sobs and cries subsided as he became exhausted. He lay limp and inert on the concrete. As his heart slowed to a more gentle rhythm, he realized that he could feel a cool movement of air on his forehead. There was a breeze or a draught from somewhere. Whatever sort of a prison this was, if air could get in, then maybe light could, too. And if light could get *in*, then maybe he could get *out*? Maybe everything just seemed so black because this was the middle of the night and morning would come. Perhaps if he made himself rest a little then, when there was more light, he could take a proper look at where he was and think clearly.

Above all, he must not let his fears overcome him. He must not let his claustrophobia claim his mind. He had to rest. He must get rid of this headache and not be too tired to find a way out of whatever predicament he was in.

Eventually, a sort of sleep claimed him, a sleep full of images. He dreamed, or did he remember? Going to the wood with Vix's evening food and the walkie-talkies for King Methwin in that strange Other World. Matt felt as high as a kite, the evening was a lark, it was a sneak-out through the attic, but there was something unusual about it... It had not been like the other times... Oh yes, Cathy lived next door now. He drifted over the events of the last few days but nothing made any sense as to why he was where he was.

At last, he found he was awake again, and beginning to think, to remember, properly. He had slid down the outhouse roof as usual, landed on a dustbin and knocked it over—that had been a close call. It had made a dreadful noise! He'd dropped Vix's food and lost half of it on the ground. He'd had to pick it up with his fingers and put it back... Ugh! Gross!

With difficulty, he lifted his fingers to his face and smelled them with disgust. As Cathy would have said, 'dogpoo stew'. That bit of his memory was right then, the smell of dogfood on his hands was pretty irrefutable evidence.

So was the fact that his hands were tied and very sore.

Matt closed his eyes and tried to remember. What had happened next? He'd gone to feed Vix as usual, then...

Then he'd seen the men! They'd started climbing the knoll just as he was scraping out the tin, so he'd dropped it and slipped further into the hazel coppice. Half his instincts told him to run, the other half to freeze. There was something unnerving about these two. They weren't insomniacs out for a midnight walk.

Who were they and what were they doing there at that time of night?

They were arguing. He could not see them; the rain-clouds hung heavily across the moon but, by their voices and glimmers from their torch, he could work out that one was older, with a stoop.

Matt remembered easing himself further back between the hazel trunks, slightly below the crest of the knoll, watching them clumsily crash their way up the steep little hill. Would they put Vix off coming for her food tonight? he wondered. He knew foxes didn't mind noise if it were familiar, like a motorway, but they hated disturbance. Vix was very timid indeed. Matt hoped she would not come.

At the top of the knoll, the men stood still, but went on arguing and swearing at each other. Matt could not help but hear every word they were saying.

'I still don't see what the fuss is about,' the younger voice moaned. 'What's half an acre? Anyway, who's going to notice? I say build on the whole plot and say nowt.'

The older voice snapped irritably. 'Honestly, Harley, I sometimes wonder if someone as dense as you can possibly be my son. 'Look!' The older man shone his torch on a map he was flapping irritably. 'Look!'

'Well, hold it still, Dad, or I can't look.'

The two men had crouched on the ground and spread the huge paper between them. 'Here, where we are now is not our land. The whole strip, from this rise to the end of Longacre Lane, belongs to the wretched farmer who owns the fields bordering the wood. If we don't build on this, we lose ten houses. If we lose that, we can't afford to pay for the land and the building materials for the other sites. It's all cut pretty close as it is, even with the nicked bricks and timber.'

'So what's the fuss?' the younger man answered. 'My mates can lift the pipes and plumbing stuff for you. It'll save a fortune, we can build on what we've got and have a nice woody bit on the side. Very classy.'

The older man sighed and stood up. 'You don't get it, do you? Owning the land is the one bit of the operation which has got to be legal, and we can't pay for it if we lose one-fifth of our profits. The money just isn't there. Hold this.' He handed the torch to his son whilst he folded the map. 'We've got to get this sorted out before next Tuesday, when the sale of the wood is completed, or we won't be able to go through with it.'

The younger man shivered. 'It's freezing out here—and it's the middle of the night! Why can't we do all this tramping about in daylight ,when we could at least see what we are doing?'

'Because when I discover that my dear son has overlooked a small detail like this at nine o'clock at night, I like to know what the damage is straight away. We've only got hours to get this right now. Apart from that, if anyone—especially that wretched farmer who own this bit—should see us poking around just here, they might put two and two together. I wish you'd shut up and let me think.'

The younger man sniffed. 'I still say you're worrying too much. Build first and let the farmer try and make us pull them down!'

The two men started the walk across the knoll towards Matt, and silently he flattened himself against the nearest tree trunk, not daring to breathe.

As he walked, the younger man shone the torch around in great sweeps as if he was trying to survey the whole area in its puny light. Matt could feel his heart pounding so loudly, he was sure they could hear it.

Just as they had almost passed him, the young man stopped. 'I know it's a daft question, Dad...'

'It usually is from you. Go on.'

'But have you actually *asked* the farmer if you can buy the land... you know, legit. and all that?'

'Yes, I rang him as soon as you told me.'

'And?'

'And the man's barmy. He says it's not for sale, the land is sacred and "the Guardian" wouldn't like it. I don't see what a flippin' newspaper has to do with it, but the guy was so obviously a nutter, I didn't see there was much point arguing... So now we've got to keep out of sight if we're on this bit of land, or he'll smell a rat. Hey, what's that?'

The swinging torchlight had flicked across Matt's terrified figure. However much he tried to look like a tree trunk, it wasn't going to work. There was only one thing for it, to run like crazy and hope to outwit them amongst the trees.

But this time, the tree roots outwitted him. He ran pell-mell down the slope so fast that he tripped and hit his head hard. For a couple of seconds, the world seemed to stop. There was no pain, no sound, nothing.

Then, suddenly, there came the crashing, throbbing agony in his head, and shouting everywhere. Then there was total blackness.

***

Matt eased his sore limbs and tried unsuccessfully to loosen the ropes that tied his hands. He had obviously been taken somewhere by the men, but where? They must have known he had heard everything. Matt tried to sit up. A faint light of grey dawn was framed by a small double window up high to his left. It was very pale and indistinct, but his hopes rose at the sight. If only he could get untied, he might be able to get out. If only his head would stop aching...

He shifted his position. Whatever had been poking in his back earlier was now hurting his hip-bone. With difficulty, he tugged at his jacket, pulling it round from underneath his side. Whatever the lump was, it was hidden in his pocket. It felt like a large rock.

With a lot of shifting and tugging he managed to open his tied hands like a duck's beak and pull out the hidden trouble-maker.

It was one of the walkie-talkies!

In the grey light he looked at it. Could it be possible that Cathy—or someone else—might find the other one? That could take days, or even weeks. Maybe the men had picked it up. What would happen to him if he tried using it? Might they be listening at the other end? Dare he try?

He pushed it behind him and lay down again, in case anyone came in to look at him. If they did not know about the walkie-talkie, they must not find out. These bits of plastic and wire might just save his life... but how long would the batteries hold, and would anyone useful find the other one?

Snare Howl

With the growing light of day a small, lithe shape slipped away from the row of semi-derelict garages.

During the night, Vix had found the scent of Boy on the knoll. At first, she had smelled fear. A little further on there was Boy's blood on the low branch. These scents left their trail through the wood and were easy to follow. On top of that, the acrid stench of the little fire-sticks the men dropped hung everywhere.

The sour rubber of warm car tyres had been more difficult to trace, once the tracks joined those of other cars on the main road.

Vix was able to tell the car had gone out of the village and turned right, but for how long? She dare not test for warmth in the middle of the road. That might have told her something, there were so few cars at that time of night. But she had seen so many of her kindred laid low by the hard and heartless hitting of these metal boxes that growled and roared, collided and killed, and then drove on relentlessly.

No, she would have to find her own way, if she

could. Anyway, the tracks were muddled with so many others that she would not be able to tell one from another.

For long, painstaking hours she limped and sniffed on one side of the road, then on the other. As she sensed the first hints of dawn breaking, Vix slipped into a large wood to lie low. She did not know the area well, and did not want the other foxes to think she was challenging their territory. She would just have a short rest while she thought about what to do.

'Why?' she pondered, 'Why should men with firesticks take Boy and make him bleed? Perhaps I should speak to Methwin.'

Just as she began to settle into a bed of young bracken, she heard a terrible howling of anguish. She shivered. She remembered her own howl when she realized she was caught in a snare and would probably die there. Boy had come to her help. She did not want to investigate this scream, although she was very curious. What animal was it? She could not recognize the cry. It was so wild and in such intense anguish, the creature would probably tear her to pieces if she got near. She could do nothing anyway, a poor lame fox with only her teeth as weapons. Teeth did not prevail against human snares. She tried to close her eyes and ignore the howling, but her own memories made her paw ache terribly.

At last, she could stand the cries no longer. Leaving her warm nest of dried ferns, she turned towards Foxdown Wood. She would go home and speak to the King. He always knew what to do. But just as she began to venture across the road, she sensed a terrible shaking and rumbling beneath her paws, and smelled the stench of fumes. There was never a smell like that in Methwin's world. Why did humans put up with it here? she wondered, but then she realized she had to concentrate. These were all the signs that something big and angry was about to come roaring along the road, something that would surely put an end to her life if she did not run away.

She jumped back just as the huge lorry came thundering past, lights blindingly bright and loud, thumping music blaring out from the cab.

Vix cowered in the hedgerow at the edge of the road. Why did humans keep such monsters? Why did they ride them? Suddenly, she felt too sick and frightened to continue. Did this wood not have a Guardian to care for it and protect it, like Foxdown did? Vix sighed. It was such a long and terrifying walk back to her home and Methwin. She felt so tired and lonely. All she wanted was someone wise and reassuring to talk to.

But if she went back to Methwin, what could he do? He had never come to this world and knew nothing of its ways. Not that Vix felt she understood half of what she saw. And Methwin could only give advice. He had too many problems of his own to come to another world to chase a scream in the night. It was only a badger caught in a trap, after all... Or was it?

Vix washed her ruffled coat with her rough tongue, and thought. If Methwin could only give advice, what would he say? To be sure, Vix did not know. All she knew was that the sound of the cry bothered her. Suddenly, she knew what she had to do. She got up, and ran towards the place where the cry had come from.

It was almost daylight before she had crossed the wood again, nibbling at a few woodlice and a mouse or two on the way. She was very hungry. She had not eaten the food on the knoll; she had been too disturbed by the smell of fear and Boy's blood to think of eating. Now she sat with the last few beech trees behind her; ahead was a rusty twisted wire fence and a clearing with low buildings and wrecks of cars. Had the cry come from this far off? Perhaps some creature had been wounded on the road and left to die? She had to know. It was still not properly day—she would be safe in human territory for a little while.

Silently she slipped under the fence and trotted past three rusty cars and a heap of engine parts. All the way she sniffed and listened. Round and round she walked, testing the air every few steps for a scent of something different, she did not know what. Perhaps fear, perhaps blood. She could not detect that any animals large enough to make such a cry had been that way for several hours.

She clambered to the top of one of the low buildings and pricked her huge ears, swinging them around to catch the slightest sound. But she heard only early morning wood sounds. Nothing was writhing in pain. There were badgers nearby, and some rabbits, some cacophonous, territory-grabbing birds and a few crows arguing over a dead rat.

But nothing that could have made that awful cry. She wanted to go home to look for Boy, yet she had to stay. Oh, why was she only an insignificant little vixen? She sat on the corrugated roof of the last of the low buildings and threw back her head and howled a cry of grief and loss and fear.

'If this wood has a Guardian, then perhaps he will tell the one that cares for our wood,' she thought.

But as she drew breath to howl a second time, she tasted something on the air. It was warm rubber! A car had been here during the night, leaving the fresh scent of tyres and exhaust fumes in the air.

Intrigued, she jumped down and began to search for the scent. Perhaps whatever had made the cry had been hit by the car. If the creature were dead, at least she could sing the dirge for the poor thing. More importantly than that, the scent was similar to the car that had taken Boy away! This was silly, she told herself. Every human car smelled like this, and lots of humans dropped fire-sticks like the ones scattered by her paws right now.

Softly, she padded around. The car had gone, but there *was* a familiar scent here... a smell of Boy!

Suddenly, she heard a small movement of something heavy being dragged across a hard floor. She listened again. There was breathing too, human breathing!

Vix looked around, terrified. The daylight was getting stronger, she really ought to be running for the shelter of the trees soon, humans might be bustling around before long. But her curiosity was too strong. She clambered up an elder bush that grew hard against the wall of the concrete building and looked through a grimy window.

There, a long leap below, was the figure of a small human, wriggling like an adder across the floor. She could not smell him because of the glass, and she could not see his face in the half-light, but she was certain it was Boy!

Vix whined and pushed at the glass with her shiny black nose. But she could do nothing. Boy could not hear her—he was too busy struggling with his bonds. She jumped down and ran backwards, forwards, and all around the building, but she could find no way in. There was nothing for it, she *would* have to go back and find Methwin.

Perhaps if she could explain things to him, he could tell the Cathy-friend where Boy was.

But how could she explain? Even in Methwin's world, she only had images in her head and no words to describe what she saw.

The Truth is Told

Cathy did not hesitate. She had barely registered that her Mum had bought a TV and video recorder, or that she was trying to be nice to her.

The shouting in the wood at the end of her garden was the calling she had subconsciously been waiting for all day. She had half guessed something was wrong, Matt should have come round during the day—if only to tell her that the Other World wasn't real. They should have shared the joke.

Although Matt had not come, Cathy had been too unwell to realize he was missing. But would she have called on him if she had realized? She had heard enough about Matt Carter's Dad and did not to want to go and knock on his door.

All anyone could have done was to wait until something happened. Now it had. Matt must have been missing all last night and all day today. She bit her lip, very angry. Why hadn't she noticed? Why hadn't she *done* something?

She grabbed her jacket and ran out into the dark.

Maggie did not know what was happening, but she understood the feeling of fear that was hanging in the night air. She also pulled a coat off the hook and followed her daughter into the garden.

'Hello, Mr Carter?' Cathy called from the end of her garden.

Harry Carter stopped dead still and peered through the inky blackness to find the unknown voice. He turned his torch towards the rustling at the bottom of the chalky bank below. The thin beam revealed a long-faced girl with straight, dark hair. She looked like a worried rabbit caught in the light. A little further off a woman's voice called, 'Cathy, where are you? What's happening? I can't see anything!'

The girl's voice called out, 'Just a sec, Mum, I'll come to you as soon as I can, stay still, there's fairly lethal barbed wire just in front of you!'

Harry waited as the tall shape clambered up the slope and stood in front of him. 'You are Mr Carter, aren't you? Matt's Dad? I heard you calling.'

'I am, but what's it to you?'

Cathy held out a muddy hand, 'I'm Cathy Mackeson. I live next door. I was worried about Matt, too. I'd expected to see him today. Where is he?'

'What's happening up there?' Maggie called out nervously.

'Look, young lady, Matt's whereabouts are nothing to do with you... unless you know something?' he added suspiciously.

Cathy could not see more than a thin tall shape in front of her, but the voice was tense and clipped. She felt most uncomfortable. 'Just let me get my Mum, will you? I might be able to help, although I don't know much.'

Harry Carter's voice was severe in the dark. 'That isn't the *proper* way up, you know—the correct way to come is along the lane.'

Cathy, who was halfway down the bank by this time, called out, 'I know, but this is a darned sight quicker! Here, Mum, follow my voice. Then feel low for my hand. There's a dip under the wire you can wriggle under. What's happening is that Matt, the newspaper boy from next door, is missing.'

'Oh my goodness!' puffed Maggie, as she reached the top of the bank. 'I'm Maggie Mackeson, Cathy's Mum. How can we help? How long has Matt been gone?'

Mr Carter seemed very irritated. 'Look ladies, I much appreciate your offers, but this really is none of your business. I can look after my own son perfectly well, and just because he's a bit late home is really no cause for concern. Now, it's a cold, dark night, why don't you just...'

'But he didn't come home after feeding Vix last night, did he?' Cathy interrupted, a sudden feeling of panic catching in her throat as she realized the implications of the untouched window-latch and the loft entrance left open.

'That fox? No, he didn't go and feed her. He was reading a magazine and hadn't done his chores when I got home from work, so I grounded him. He went to bed early...'

'And he wasn't in the house this morning,' Cathy finished for him. She could sense Matt's Dad's irritation. She knew more about him than his Dad did. He was angry and she felt powerful. She was going to press home the fact that he didn't communicate with his son, and there was lots he didn't know about Matt. Cathy was raring for a fight. After all, it was his Dad's fault that Matt was missing. If he'd taken the trouble to be interested in what Matt did, her friend might not be missing now!

She felt Mr Carter staring at her, although she could see nothing in the blackness. The jumbled light from his torch twitched across roots and bushes by his feet. The man's movements were sharp and frantic.

Suddenly, Cathy felt sorry for him. He was scared. She ought to help rather than pick on him. She softened her voice. 'I know where Matt goes to feed the fox... and he *did* go last night.'

As soon as she said it, Cathy regretted it. She would have to tell Mr Carter *how* Matt escaped once he'd been sent to bed. She hadn't meant to betray her friend, but this was too important. She felt terribly torn. She had too many conflicting emotions all at once.

'Of course Matt didn't go out last night,' Mr Carter snapped. 'Not only would he not dream of disobeying me, but once the door is bolted, it's too stiff for him to open. Even *I* struggle with it. Now I'll thank you to leave me to my own business, Goodnight!' he snapped and started to march away.

Cathy decided she would have to tell the truth. Matt was her only friend, and he might be in serious trouble. She called out after him. 'Please believe me! Matt did go out last night—he went through your attic, into ours, then out through my bedroom window.'

Maggie laughed. 'So that's what the dreadful clattering was in the middle of the night. I wondered what you were up to!'

Mr Carter seemed to believe Cathy at last. He stopped and turned around, the bright light of the torch swinging as he did so. 'Well, he won't do it again. I'll see to that!' And he slapped his thigh with his hand in a threatening way. 'I did not bring my son up to go into young girl's bedrooms in the middle of the night... I'm horrified!'

'But it wasn't like that, it was just an escape route...' Cathy began, horrified that she had opened up such a hornet's nest of problems for poor Matt.

'He had nothing to escape *from*, I assure you...' Mr Carter said tersely, marching on again.

Maggie sensed the tension in Cathy's lack of reply, and ran after her unseen neighbour. 'Look, Mr Carter, Cathy said she knows where Matt usually goes. Don't you think we ought to go there first, to see if there are any clues before we worry about the whys and where-fores?'

Mr Carter stood still again and sighed. 'I suppose so. If you do know something I ought to hear it, but I assure you that I will have words with that boy when he comes home. Going through your bedroom indeed!'

'Let's not worry about that. Let's just see what we can find,' Maggie coaxed gently.

Mr Carter just 'humphed' and followed after Cathy as she picked her way expertly through the wood.

'I think it was rather funny, really,' whispered Maggie, making Cathy chuckle. She smiled at her Mum for the first time in many months, only it was too dark for Maggie to see.

At the hazel coppice, there was a dirty fork and a half-empty dog food tin. 'I'll have words with that boy,'

Mr Carter started moaning again. 'I'm not having him littering, it's just not done. He'll have to stop feeding that disgustingly smelly animal, anyway. They will take him into care if they think I let him near dirty animals. They'll say I can't look after him, and I'm not having it, I'm really not!'

Maggie glanced at the tall thin shape beside her. So that was it, he had to be a perfect Dad because someone had threatened him... poor man... poor Matt! No wonder the boy had fled. She stared at the ground as Mr Carter shone his torch around.

'He's not here. We really won't be able to find anything else tonight. We'd better go back and ring the police,' Maggie said.

Mr Carter snapped irritably. 'No. I'm not having that. He's gone to stay with a friend. Yes, I'm sure that's it...' And with that he shone his torch over towards Longacre Lane. 'That's the *proper* way back, by the way,' he informed everyone tersely, and strode off in that direction, marching in stony silence.

'Come on, Mum, we'll be home first,' Cathy grabbed her Mum's hand and led her through the undergrowth almost as expertly as Matt might have done. As she passed the little hollow where they had played going to the Other World with the fox, she glimpsed, or thought she glimpsed, a flash of light from under the tree roots. But a scrambling of claws and a short, rough bark distracted her.

It was Vix, scurrying away as fast as she could!

For the first time, the kitchen of Knighthayes Cottage felt warm and cosy and welcoming to Cathy. She made some tea and sat down opposite her Mum.

'Matt really did go through my bedroom last night

to feed Vix—the little fox that lives in the woods. She has a front paw missing and couldn't fend for herself if she wasn't fed you see... Matt's been looking after her for ages. She's his only friend, he doesn't get on well with his Dad. He has to have escape places. He has his own world up there.' Cathy bit her tongue. She had said things she had not meant to, but in a way she was pleased with herself. She couldn't have been more honest—nor could she have put things better if she had tried.

Maggie did not seem the slightest bit thrown. 'I can see why he needs all that,' she answered as she poured more tea. 'I used to do much the same when I was a child,' she stopped and grinned. 'It was enormous fun!'

'Was that when you lived with the Aunts in Bexhill-on-Sea?'

'Not half! And it would have been sheer misery if I hadn't had my own little world to run to!'

Cathy hesitated and looked sideways at her mother, 'You—you mean a sort of *Other World?*'

'Yes, that's it exactly! I never told anyone, obviously. But I've never quite believed it wasn't real.' Maggie sat looking dreamy with her chin on her hand. She seemed to look a lot younger suddenly, and very far away.

Cathy sat silently in amazement. She could think of nothing to say. The thought of her Mum having ever been to an 'Other World' did not seem to make sense. She was suspicious. Was she just trying to be nice to her? To get her to trust her and talk to her?

Suddenly Maggie sat up straight and looked serious and grown-up again. 'But meanwhile, what are we going to do about Matt? I don't feel I can ring the police without Mr Carter's permission.'

'We can't do anything,' Cathy shrugged, dismissively. She felt suspicion and anger closing in around her again. She felt uneasy with the feeling of trust and confidence that had crept into the evening. 'I'm going to bed—I still don't feel well.'

In the dark, Cathy lay awake, waiting for the sounds that would tell her Mum had settled for the night. 'Give it an hour,' she thought. 'Once Mum's asleep, I know *exactly* what I'm going to do.'

An Unfriendly
Welcome

As the early-morning half light began to make the world seem blue everywhere, a dark figure slipped under the barbed wire and scrambled up the bank. Cathy did not take much trouble to be quiet. She had no idea she was being followed.

All she could think of was the barmy idea that was rattling around in her head. That momentary flash of light between the tree roots had made her think. Perhaps she had been hasty, perhaps the Other World *was* real after all, but she just hadn't quite hit the entrance—or perhaps the fox had to be there to open the way.

Anyway, she would go and look for Matt without Mr Walking-Corpse next door interfering. Matt was her friend and, in his funny way, he had been good to her. He'd trusted her with his fox, and given her something for herself, something outside home and the miserable anger she felt deep inside.

If it took all night and all day, she'd look until she found some clue as to where Matt had gone. He would *never* have left an empty can around in the wood. Vix might have pushed her nose inside to lick the last bits of food, and she then would have been cut all around her muzzle. No. Something had happened to make him leave the copse quickly!

If that glimpse of light she had seen as the fox ran out of the hollow had shone through a chink between the Other World to this, perhaps Matt was there. He had intended to go through to take the walkie-talkies to the King after all. There was no way she could try and explain all this Other World nonsense to her Mother, despite what she had said about her own pretend world. Even if King Methwin and everything was just a game, it was an important one that might give a clue to where Matt was now.

At first, the soft, leafy floor of the wood muffled the sound of the second figure as it stalked Cathy's footsteps. As they made their way deeper into the wood, snapping twigs underfoot made Cathy stop short and stare around. The second figure melted into the shadow of a tree trunk.

But she forgot everything as a pale, ghostly shape suddenly swept down in front of her. She gave a sharp gasp, and then breathed again as she realized that the wide, outstretched wings carried the short, round barrel of a large barn owl, which swept right past her face and then disappeared into the night.

Then a short, coughing bark, probably from Vix, brought Cathy back to the present. She took a few more tentative steps and listened. Nothing. It was getting lighter all the time, she would feel safer then. The semi-luminous blue light was giving way to greys and deep greens. She tripped over a tree root and fell face down in the cold, wet, slimy bluebell leaves. For a second, she thought she saw a movement behind her—her spine prickled and she felt the tiny muscles on her scalp lifting her hair.

She was cold, lonely, and was beginning to feel frightened as well. She glanced around. She was fairly sure that the hollow was not far away. Ahead and slightly to her left, huge black shapes loomed like frozen waves of the sea.

Just then a soft intake of breath behind her confirmed that she *was* being followed, and by a human, not a fox. She would have to run for it and just hope that the way through to Methwin's world was open, or that at least she could hide in the tree-root tunnel until the follower lost her and went away.

Cathy could feel her heart rate rising, her breathing became shallow and fast as the adrenalin surged into her blood. Glancing around one more time, she gathered all her reserves of strength and courage and then, scrambling to her feet, she flung herself at the tree roots, leaped over a rotten bough and jumped quite blindly into the hollow at the other side.

Frantically, she groped around for the entrance to the gap, kicking at odd branches and damp piles of leaves as she felt for a way through. Above her, footsteps ran crashing, no longer secretive.

Cathy flattened herself under the protectively knotted fingers of the tree roots as a human shape, dark and undefined, jumped down into the hollow behind her. She screamed as she was landed on clumsily and painfully, and then propelled into... the arms of a very tall, handsome middle-aged woman with flame-red hair and arms like tree trunks.

Another pair of arms caught Cathy's pursuer as she tumbled through the tunnel. There, firm in the grip of a tall, fair man was... Mum!

For a moment, Cathy stared in horror and surprise at her mother. Then she collected her wits and began to wriggle and squirm for all she was worth. But the enormous woman just laughed, so Cathy let herself hang loose as if she had given up resistance. At this, her captor relaxed and loosened her grasp just as Cathy ducked low and slipped out from the woman's arms, delivering several sharp karate kicks as she did so. The well-positioned edges of her feet caught sharply against her victim's unprotected shins, making the woman leap away in agony.

Maggie, who had not been so lucky with her captor, stamped very hard on his feet, but she was not a heavy woman, and her trainers did no damage, except to make the man laugh and hold her even more tightly.

Cathy's warrior woman was recovering her composure, and sprang at Cathy, just as she was moving in to attack the man who held her mother. She turned at Maggie's warning shout and moved sideways, so the woman head-butted her companion instead of Cathy.

The huge blond man did not loosen his grasp, although he was knocked to the ground by the force of the blow. The woman rolled sideways and sprang to her feet again. Crouching very low to match Cathy's height, she glowered dangerously as she unsheathed a heavy broadsword from her side and grasped it in both hands.

Cathy glanced from side to side. Where could she

stand without tripping? Where were there clear areas? What was the man doing who held Mum? Too many questions, and no time to work out any answers! She had to concentrate and eyeball this furious woman, whose square face now flamed almost as red as her tightly-bound hair.

Cathy watched the woman measure her balance, and gently move the sword hilt from her right hand to her left, then back again. Which hand was she going to use? Oh, please, may she not be ambidextrous! Cathy glanced up; the sun was high, and that was to her disadvantage. If the woman drew herself to her full height, Cathy would have to look up, and that might dazzle her.

Slowly, with mincing, dancing steps, feigning indecision, Cathy moved away from her aggressor, pretending to be looking for an escape, but all the time gently moving around so her back was to the sun. The woman snorted, showing strong, white teeth. Cathy felt cold, but she had to keep her head.

The sword flashed as it was raised. Cathy danced to the right, avoiding the blow. The blade hit the chalky earth with a clang, raising white dust in the summer air.

Grasping the hilt more firmly, the woman swung it again, but lower this time, and in a left-to-right sweep. Cathy jumped high, and felt the blade catch her shoe. This was enough to make her landing awkward, so she rolled tightly, avoiding the inevitable follow-up thrust.

Scrambling to her feet, Cathy was getting worried. She was hot and thirsty, and now she was facing the sun again. Once more, she tried to manoeuvre the woman to face the other way, but the strange warrior was getting irritated and angry by now, swinging the sword hard, with lunges to left and right and heavy slicing blows in between.

Cathy weighed up the odds.

Poor.

She was good at karate, for a beginner, but could not get close enough to the woman to touch her. The great arms were so long, and her reach was added to by a sword at least half her own height again.

Behind her, she could hear her mother shouting something, but could not make out what she was saying. Her heart was pounding so loudly, nothing made any sense.

Her only hope was to use her size and comparative lightness, and run. Where to? Back to the tunnel maybe? Or, if she couldn't make that, she could try to climb the nearest tree. It would not save her skin, but it might let her get her breath back and think.

With a sudden burst of terrified energy, she turned and sprinted in the direction of the wood.

But before she got there, she heard her mother shout again.

'STOP!'

Harawed

Cathy stood still, staring in amazement. She had got over the shock of the 'stalker' in the wood being her mother, only to have the bigger shock of seeing Maggie as she looked now.

She was on her feet, standing erect and proud. Still the same short, slim, dark haired Mum, dressed in jeans and tartan jacket, but her head was thrown back and she had a very un-Mumish air about her. She looked, well, regal was the only word Cathy could think of.

Maggie's captor had let her go and another tall, very handsome man, almost two metres high, with dark eyes and tanned skin, was striding across to them.

A band of warriors waited at a respectful distance, more like a guard of honour than attackers.

Cathy's adversary put up her sword and grasped Cathy firmly by the back of the neck as she marched her across to the dark-eyed man and Maggie.

Cathy was ignored. The man, who, from the look of his heavy gold arm bands and rings, appeared to be a prince, was quite engrossed with her mother. He gave a sweeping bow and kissed her hand. His voice was as smooth as his manners: 'My word, it is the Lady Margaret herself! Have you changed your mind to come back and marry me after all these years, my dear?'

Mum shook her head. 'Not this time, Lord Harawed. This was an… unplanned visit.'

Still shaken from the effort of the fight, Cathy blinked and opened her mouth in amazement, for her own mother seemed quite at home, even honoured, here. She *had* been to another world before, *this one*!

'And who is this at your side, a serving wench?' Harawed continued.

'That's right!' Maggie threw a warning glance at Cathy to be quiet. 'We were chasing a runaway slave, a lanky boy with red hair—have you seen him? Never mind, he is stupid and of not much value to me. We lost him by the wood behind us and found ourselves here by accident.'

Harawed shook his head. 'No, but there are so many riff-raff around these parts these days, I may well have missed him.'

Cathy frowned. Mum was talking such nonsense. She may have been here before, but she had obviously forgotten that Harawed or whatever his name was would *hear* the lies her mother was telling? Methwin said that people spoke with the heart in this land.

Harawed did not seem overly concerned. He merely clapped his hands and summoned his servants to give refreshment to his guests.

'Forgive my warriors' lack of gentle reception, My Lady,' he bowed again. 'As I am sure you will recall, my people are superstitious, and believe that the wood is... shall we say, haunted? Anyone who comes from that place is immediately regarded with suspicion. I will, of course, have these warriors' hands cut off for their mistreatment of you.'

Maggie bowed in response. 'Pray, do not distress yourself, My Lord! Your warriors were doing their duty to the best of their ability. It was, in any case, thoughtless of me to rush from the wood in such a manner. I was so intent on following my slave that I gave no thought to the ancient stories of this place. Furthermore, your warriors might not have recognized me, it is many years since I came to these parts. Let them go.'

'As you wish,' Harawed smiled. Cathy thought he looked smarmy. She hoped her Mum wasn't *really* thinking of marrying this man. Apart from everything, Mum was still technically married to Dad.

Harawed moved away, and began to talk with a huge, fair woman, clad in heavy leather armour. She looked like a warrior chief. She glowered every so often in their direction. As servants came and went, setting out the picnic food, Cathy managed to whisper, 'What *are* you doing? Why were you following me?'

Maggie picked damp leaves out of her dark hair and brushed the dust from her clothes as she sat herself comfortably down by the linen cloth that had been spread in the shade of a few young beech trees. 'I was worried about Matt. I had a feeling you knew something, and I thought you might want help, so I followed you. Anyway, I'm sorry if I'm in the way, I didn't mean any harm. I know it's your adventure and your world now.'

Cathy did not know whether she was pleased to have her Mum there, or angry that the adventure was no longer her and Matt's secret, but she was too busy biting into fresh bread to be able to answer. Maggie made a wry face. 'I just had to do something. Mr Carter wasn't exactly easy, was he? Matt'll never be found if things are left to him.'

'S'pose not,' Cathy muttered, with her mouth full. She was still finding it difficult to come to terms with her mother being *here*, and what was worse, knowing more about it than she did.

Then, as if Maggie was reading her daughter's thoughts, she hugged her knees and looked around. 'I suppose you'll never believe this, but I'm certain this is the world where I used to go when I was your age. For many years I had thought it was a game, but either you and I are sharing a dream, or it is real—in a way. Anyway, when I was younger, I knew this man well. He's a scoundrel of the first order, but in his world I am a princess and outrank him quite nicely. I don't want him to know you are my daughter, in case things go badly and he kidnaps you. So far, I think I can talk us out of whatever we have walked into. I don't want to have to bargain for our lives at *this* stage!'

Cathy was confused. 'But you were in Bexhill-on-Sea, and this is Knapsden. How could it be the same place?'

'Distance and place are different in worlds like this. I'm not sure if it is the same *place*, but these are most certainly the same people!'

Above them, the midsummer sun shone hot and bright. Everywhere the field grass was dotted with bright blue wild chicory. Ahead was a gaudy array of small, many-coloured pavilion tents. Harawed seemed lost in conversation with his warriors, glancing round occasionally, and stroking his clean-shaven chin as he looked at the Lady Margaret and her girl.

Cathy bit into a succulent peach and wiped at the dribbling juices. 'But why the part about Matt being a runaway slave?'

Maggie smiled. 'It was just a wild guess that he might be here, too. If they think there are more of us, they may conclude we are spies. If we are merely after a slave (who wouldn't count to a vain man like Harawed), we might be able to carry this charade off and get back to the wood.'

'Well, he might not be with this man, there's another place on the other side of the wood...' Cathy tried to explain, but Maggie stopped her. 'Shhh! He's watching us. Tell me when we're away from here.'

Cathy nodded. She was beginning to enjoy herself. The fruit and soft breads spread before them made an excellent breakfast, especially when washed down with honey-sweetened water.

Maggie did not relax. She watched Harawed's every movement warily. Now he and his followers were obviously discussing the unexpected visitors. Maggie leaned across to Cathy, whispering, I think we're in for trouble. I wish I had a scimitar in my hand—I'm beginning to feel edgy.'

Cathy stole a glance at her comfortable Mum, dressed in jeans that had seen better days, a faded jogging top and a padded tartan jacket. Then she looked at the warriors, their huge billowing white shirts under short, tightly fitted scarlet and vermilion coats, wide loose trousers and long hair tied back in pony-tails. Somehow, the thought of Mum dressed as one of them, heavy curved sword in hand, did not quite work.

She giggled, but then caught her mother's eye. There was a dignity and sternness there she had never noticed before. Suddenly she *could* imagine her as a warrior princess with a golden circlet in her hair and jewelled armbands above her elbows.

'Why a scimitar, Mum? Why not a long sword like the others?'

Maggie laughed and stretched out her arms. 'Look at my wrists compared to theirs! I couldn't even lift one of their broadswords, let alone wield it without cutting off my own toes!'

Just then she stopped laughing and jumped to her feet, serious suddenly. 'Time to get out of here. Keep quiet and do as I say; I think things are getting dangerous.'

Cathy looked around, most of the warriors were gathering round them, but they all had their arms folded as if they were waiting. They looked determined, but not as if they were about to fight.

Maggie held out her arms welcomingly as Harawed approached. '*Dear* Prince Harawed, *please* forgive me, but I must be going. Thank you *so* much for your hospitality. My missing slave is *such* a nuisance; I must capture him before he gets too far. Would your warriors mind escorting myself and my maid to help in the recapture? And,' she added softly, so only Harawed could hear, 'I would so like to see you again, I will return.'

Harawed had obviously not expected this. His thick eyebrows shot up and he looked pleased. Then he clapped his hands and summoned two of his followers, a black-haired woman and a younger, fair boy.

He took Maggie's hands, made an elaborate bow and kissed her. 'You will be back tonight?'

'I will make every effort to be back tonight,' she replied. 'We have been apart so long...' She lingered, looking into his eyes and smiling, then turned and followed the warriors out of the camp towards the wood.

'I believe the wretched slave may be in the wood. He was last seen running into it, but from the other side,' Maggie called out as she skilfully manoeuvred the warriors to the left-hand side of the wood. Once they were out of sight, she and Cathy stepped into the 'haunted' shadows where no warrior of Harawed's would dare venture, towards the great fallen oaks and the tunnel which made the way home.

As they scrambled out of the other end, Maggie grabbed at some brushwood and branches to block the gap, lest any glimpse of something the other end might tempt the warriors to follow. The thought of such enormously tall and strangely-dressed people wandering the streets of Knapsden made the mind boggle.

Maggie pulled herself out of the hollow and sat on one of the tree trunks at the top. Cathy followed her and breathed the early morning air of Oxfordshire with relief.

'Well!' said Cathy, 'What was all that about?'

Maggie laughed and pushed a strand of stray hair behind her ear. 'I told you I had my own world when I lived with the dreaded Aunts after Mum and Dad died. I never thought I would see it again. I thought it had gone for ever by the time I was about fifteen.

'Harawed is the nephew of a great and powerful king, who adopted me as his daughter. That makes me a princess and him only an earl. Harawed always wanted to marry me, I suspect so he could secure the throne for himself, but I never would... I never felt I really belonged there, if you know what I mean.

'I hoped that if Harawed thought I was coming back to see him tonight, he might let me go, and I was right. He always spent more time on his looks than on sharpening his brain. Consequently, he never was very clever!' She laughed, then looked Cathy in the eye. 'But I see you are no stranger there yourself?'

Cathy blushed. 'No, I've been there once, with Matt. We met an ageing King called Methwin, who must have looked a lot like Harawed when he was younger. He said his nephew was plotting to overthrow him and that he was an evil man. But Methwin was nice. I liked him.'

Maggie nodded. 'I know Methwin. He is my adoptive father, and he is a good man. You're right. I'm sorry Harawed is giving him trouble. If it's not butting in on your adventure, I would like to help. I owe Methwin a great deal, and I am very fond of him, and I may be able to help—I am a trained warrior in that land, and I may be able to distract Harawed if I pretend I like him a little.'

'But won't he be able to hear if you're not telling the truth?'

'Because people speak with the heart in that place? Maybe, but Harawed tells so many lies he can't discern what other people are saying either. Anyway, I did not lie, I said I'd like to see him again, and I would—in prison where he belongs. And I would very much like to take part in his capture, and tonight would do just fine. I'm not doing anything else. Are you?'

There was enough light to see clearly now, although it was still a dull, misty morning.

'Matt was going to go through to Methwin's world on Friday night when he disappeared,' Cathy explained. 'I had hoped he might be there and not lost at all. Methwin was desperate for something called "words of strength" from our world, to help him in his fight against Harawed. I thought it was a sort of magic, but Matt was going to give Methwin his walkie-talkies, so that he could communicate with his other commanders so they could come and rescue him. He thought that might make Methwin's words stronger. But I've no idea whether Matt got this far or not. I can't see any footprints down here. It's too chalky.'

Maggie looked around; there were no tell-tale marks of any kind. How would they know if Matt had been that way at all?

'I don't think Matt got as far as going through the tunnel,' Maggie said, thoughtfully. 'Harawed's patrols would have seen him if he had. They pounced on us quickly enough. Harawed would have been only too glad to have handed the boy over—to win my favour if nothing else. And for once I don't think he was lying.'

Cathy stood up and stretched. 'Let's go back to the knoll where we found the empty tin. If he didn't get as far as the tunnel to the Other World, he must have left the wood from there.' They started walking silently through the wood, peering this way and that for the slightest clues.

'There are a lot of gun cartridges over there,' Maggie pointed to an untidy heap of what looked like discarded red plastic cigarettes, a little to their right.

'Some poor partridge will be on someone's plate tonight.'

As they approached the knoll, they stopped and looked all around. 'It's hopeless!' Cathy moaned, kicking irritably at the heaps of rotting leaves from last autumn drifted, like piles of rusted snow, at the side of the path. 'How do we find anything in this lot? Are you sure Matt hasn't gone through and Harawed is just holding him to see what he can get out of him?'

'I suppose anything is possible. But what do you think *that* is? That black thing by your right foot?

Vix Tries to
Explain

The walkie-talkie was rather damp, but it crackled into life as Cathy pressed the switch.

'Matt? Matt? Are you there?'

Nothing.

'Let's go back towards the tunnel,' Maggie suggested, 'It's nearer the edge of the wood, and there might be less interference.'

'Do trees make any difference?' Cathy had never been much good at science.

'I don't know, but it's worth a try.'

As they walked along, they tried the walkie-talkie, but apart from a slight crackle, there was no response.

'Perhaps Matt hasn't got his switched on?' Cathy suggested. They were so engrossed in what they were doing, that neither Cathy nor her Mum noticed that they were not alone in the wood.

'Oi! You there, this wood is private property!'

A thin, grey-haired man with a stoop was standing

only a few metres away and, next to him, a younger man with a shotgun.

'Terribly sorry,' Maggie tried being conciliatory. 'We're new around here, we didn't know. Would you be so kind as to tell us the quickest way to leave your property, and we'll be gone.' She smiled her sweetest smile.

But it didn't work.

'What has that kid got there?' snarled the young man with a pinched, stoat-like look.

'Give it here,' the older man motioned. 'Hand it over—it looks like you've been stealing as well.'

Cathy pushed the walkie-talkie back into her pocket and looked at her mother who had gone quite white and, for the first time in her life, was lost for words. No laughter, no quick replies, just real fear.

Cathy came to her rescue. 'No scimitars here, Mum.'

Maggie shook her head. 'They're against the law, unfortunately,' she whispered. 'Bother!'

Suddenly a small, russet-brown shape darted across their path and dived under the tree roots. The younger man raised his gun and fired a shot after Vix.

'It's *you* that left all the cartridges around!' Maggie challenged, eyes glaring. She hated all blood sports.

'And what is it to you?' he asked, reloading and raising the barrels threateningly. 'Now are you going to hand over whatever it is you have there? Or am I going to have to take it from you?'

'What do I do, Mum?' Cathy whispered, hardly able to breathe.

'Down the hole—I think,' she replied, dubiously. The gateway to the Other World was still open. Warm summer air streamed up at them as they jumped into the dip and back through the tunnel. As they did so, some gunshot landed by Maggie's heel... and an arrow skimmed past Cathy's nose.

'Out of the frying-pan, into the proverbial fire,' Maggie muttered, dragging Cathy back into the bushes to the side of the tunnel entrance. Vix was cowering there too. Cathy glanced over her left shoulder to the tangle of fallen tree roots. There was no sign of a way back to their own world. The tunnel of roots had 'closed' behind them.

'Don't worry,' Vix said, peering up at the two humans with her sparkling, warm amber eyes. 'The Guardian won't let them through. They'll never find it. Meanwhile, I am so glad I found you, you are sorely needed here. The King is hard pressed by his nephew: reinforcements from an unfriendly neighbouring kingdom have arrived. Methwin summoned me to find you and bring the words of strength from your world.'

Cathy pulled the walkie-talkie from her jacket pocket and looked at it ruefully. 'I'm afraid it's not going to be much use, you see...'

Suddenly, there were terrible shouts and more arrows fell like a shower of deadly rain, only a few metres from where they were hiding. Warriors were running in all directions, wielding spears and huge, long broadswords. They were howling like hunting wolves as they ran. Some were dressed in red, and others in forest green. There was such a whirlwind between them that the onlookers could not see who was winning.

From the light and the state of the battle, it seemed that much had happened since they had left this place only a short time before. 'It always seems that you have been here the same length of time as passes at home, Maggie whispered, but for some reason I've never worked out, when you are *not* here, time travels at its own speed. It is quite unreliable and *most* inconvenient.'

Vix looked slightly quizzically at Maggie. 'You have been here before? That is why I smelled something familiar when I first saw you!'

Maggie stared at the fox, quite unperturbed at hearing her speak. Then she crouched so she could look more comfortably into Vix's golden eyes. 'I have been here, but sadly I do not remember you. Please forgive my discourtesy.'

Vix pushed her black, wet nose into Maggie's hand, and licked the skin. 'No,' she said after a few moments, 'We have not met before, but I think animals and humans who have been to Methwin's land just have a smell or a feel about them that others recognize.'

'I'm sure you are right,' Maggie began to say, for she had sensed something different about Cathy after her first visit. But now was not the time to think about such things, for the battle was moving towards the edge of the wood. The clash of swords and the shouting of the warriors was becoming more urgent. Cathy jumped back as an arrow landed very near to where they were crouched. The fox jumped further into the undergrowth and began barking urgently.

'Come,' said Vix. 'Follow me. I will take you to Methwin. They will not follow us through the wood— they are scared of it and, with those long blades, they like to fight in the open.'

Ten minutes' speedy scrambling led them to the other side of the wood and within a short run to

Methwin's gatehouse.

Smoke was curling over from behind the palisade and the sounds of fearful shouting had faded. As they stepped out of the trees, the sight of dead and wounded bodies and the smell of smoke and blood made their eyes smart and their stomachs churn.

'Now run, humans!' demanded Vix. 'Let us be fleet of paw, and may the Guardian of all go with us.'

Cathy did not take time to think; she simply belted as fast as she could across the clearing, hearing her mother's heavier footsteps close behind her. She ignored the challenges of the few remaining warriors, darting under their lethal swings of spear and sword, and landed at last, heaving for air and hammering on the thick wooden door of the gate.

'Who is it?' demanded a gruff voice from inside.

'It's Cathy... the girl from the Other World.'

'I don't know what you're talking about!'

'It is I, Vix the fox.'

'How do I know that?' was the response.

Maggie turned and saw, to her horror, a fresh band of scarlet-apparelled warriors approaching. 'Let us in!' she demanded. 'It's the Lady Margaret. I wish to see my father!'

Suddenly, the door gave under their frantic hands, swinging open and creaking, stiff on its hinges. Inside the courtyard was destruction beyond belief. The main wall of the longhouse ahead had been scorched by fire, and the thatch on the lodge roof was well ablaze. Wounded warriors lay in huddles, as the healers came to each of them in turn. Everywhere, there was despair and misery.

As the gates swung shut, Methwin himself ran

forward to greet his adoptive daughter. He no longer wore his great rich green cloak, but was dressed in stained leather armour and a dusty shirt and boots.

His huge arms encircled Maggie and, giant of a man as he was, he wept openly. 'My child, I thought I would never see you again!'

'I have been with my own people, My Lord, but I promised you I would come if ever you needed me, and I am here!' and she hugged him so hard, that even he found it hard to breathe, barrel-chested as he was. At last Maggie let him go, and introduced Cathy as, 'My daughter, the Lady Catherine.'

'Ah yes!' said the King, the child that was going to bring me the ancient words of strength. This battle will gain nothing. What have you brought, Catherine?'

Cathy hung her head. 'Nothing, My Lord.'

The king reddened and stood towering over Cathy. She felt very small indeed. 'Well,' she hesitated. 'I did, sort of,' and she explained about Matt and the walkie-talkies. 'But I am afraid that one won't work, even if you had batteries, which I don't expect you have?' she looked up, hopefully.

The King shook his head. He crossed his arms and glowered down at Cathy, letting his long silver beard-plaits fall over his chest. He looked more like a head-master than ever before. 'I thought you were going to help, but you have been weak, it seems.'

Maggie rummaged in her pocket and held out a little mirror, 'She is only a child, Father, and the idea was a good one. Instead of walkie-talkies, we could this to flash messages to your generals across the field of battle.'

'But how would they understand these messages?'

Maggie explained about Morse code, but the King pushed the little mirror away. 'My men do not know the letters and dots and dashes you speak of, and we cannot reach them to explain your code. The day is almost ended now, and we are weary and in great grief. If we can beat this attack back, all will be quiet for the night. We need something stronger, we need the ancient words. You must bring us help tomorrow, without fail.'

Cathy and Maggie looked at each other. Maggie shrugged. 'We will try, but it would help if we had more idea of what you need. We have so many words in our world, it's often difficult to sift out the strong ones from the words that are spoken just for the sake of it. Technology helps in sending the words, of course, but that's not what you want, is it?'

The king stroked his long, plaited beard and thought. 'And technology is like this little speaking box here? It all needs batteries to give it strength?'

Cathy felt red, and as if she had failed, although she knew she had done nothing wrong. 'Yes, My Lord. Matt, you know, the Boy, he thought if you could communicate with your war lords in your city you might be rescued.'

'True.' The King paused to wipe the blood from the face of a warrior woman brought in on a stretcher. 'But then that is not what I need. The stories of our ancient ones tell of strange sights that come from the woods, great beasts of power and words of strength. In our tales we are told that at the time of need these great things happen. But perhaps they were the workings of the Guardian, and it comes from a world other than yours.' He hung his head and looked quite desolate.

Vix stood on her hind legs and licked the King's hands kindly. 'I am sorry, My Lord.'

Suddenly Methwin looked up, 'Where is the Boy, Matt?' he demanded sharply. 'Has he gone over to the enemy? Why is he not here?'

Vix yelped as if her tail had been trodden on. 'I have seen him, at least I think it is him, but I do not have the words to tell you where. I have tried to get to you many times today, but I have always been beaten back by Harawed's men.'

Vix sat up straight. She took a deep breath. 'The Boy—Matt, he is in a cage!'

Cathy knelt down and put her arm around the fox's rough, bracken-red hair. 'I'm sorry, my Lord, I fear Vix is right. We think Matt has been captured by the enemy in our world—the men who want to rip up Foxdown Wood and turn it into a housing estate.'

Vix nuzzled Cathy's chin. Her warm breath made the girl feel better. 'I smelled blood and fear in the wood,' the fox went on, 'and I smelled the same men who threw burning stones at us just now. I think they must have chased Boy until he fell, then they pushed him into the back of their red, shiny box that goes fast and squashes us.'

Cathy and Methwin looked bemused. Maggie nodded. 'Burning stones must be bullets—they were shooting at us too—and the shiny box that squashes foxes is a car. Did you see this, Vix?'

'No, but I smelled it, and I know the men have a red... car,' she pronounced the word carefully. 'I followed them until I heard a great howling in the night, I followed the sound and saw what I think was Boy on the ground in a cage.'

'Where was this?' Maggie urged. 'We must go and help him.'

Vix hung her fine, pointed head. 'I have no words to tell you where. I am sad.'

Cathy stroked the fox and patted her on the back gently. 'Never mind. Can you take us there?'

Vix blinked with her great, wide amber eyes, as tears welled up. 'I do not know. I took a way through the woods under roots and through disused earths. This will be harder than digging for worms in a great frost.'

'Never mind,' Maggie said softly. 'You have been a brave and faithful fox, Vix. I'm sure we will find a way. We will talk soon about what we can do.'

Vix looked sadly into Maggie's face. 'I hope so. I love my Boy.'

Methwin turned away from his friends and stroked his beard in silence. The air was filled with the shouts of people trying to put out the flames and the moans of the injured, but Methwin simply closed his eyes and thought.

Suddenly he clapped his hands. 'I have it! As our worlds are so closely interlinked, the loss of Matt must have caused the terrible turn in our events this morning. Lady Margaret, Lady Catherine, you must go back to your world and find your friend. While you have lost hope, ours is gone too. We will just have to trust that the Guardian will provide his own Words of Strength that always came to us in ancient times.'

Maggie looked around and shook her head. 'I am not going, Father. Cathy can do all that is needed there, if Vix will guide her home. I will stay and help with your wounded. I know a little of the healing arts; I am what is called a nurse in my world. Cathy, call the police, tell them what you know, and tell Matt's Dad too. I will be back later. Hurry. I believe Methwin is right; the fate of this world hangs on what happens in ours.'

For once, Cathy did not argue. Methwin gripped her hands and shook them warmly. 'May the Guardian protect you,' he said. Then he turned, and went back to help his people.

Vix and Cathy were alone. Evening was coming on, the light was fading, and the shouts from outside had all but stopped. Just then the main gate creaked open, and a few dozen weary warriors straggled in, cold, tired and wounded.

The fox and the girl looked at each other. 'We must hurry! Try not to slip on the blood,' Vix barked. Then they sidled out of the gate and ran.

Vix Shows the Way

When Cathy arrived home, the police were already there. Harry Carter had at last decided to report Matt's disappearance. They were waiting to talk to her and her mother about when they had last seen him.

'Mum's a nurse and she's out on an emergency job helping a friend. She'll be back soon,' Cathy told them truthfully. Then she reported the sergeant how Matt and she had been planning to go to the woods, but he had to stay in to do household jobs. He had sneaked out late at night to feed his fox and she hadn't seen him since. She said nothing about the Other World, of course. No one would have believed her and, anyway, from what Vix had said, he wasn't far away.

Then she described the men in the wood who had threatened her and the fox with a shotgun. She told how she had seen them up in the wood before and had overheard their plans to build the new houses and leave the country.

'Do you think they've got Matt?' she asked, hoping to drop helpful hints from Vix's story. 'Perhaps they've got him locked up somewhere?'

The policeman smiled. 'He's probably sulking at a friend's house, as his Dad thinks. Don't you worry dear, he'll be fine.' Cathy felt herself go bright red with anger. How dare he be so patronizing! She longed to give him a jolly good kick! Time was everything for Matt. They had to get to him soon. She had to convince them what she said was true!

The sergeant was talking into his high-powered radio, and asked for the names and addresses of the developers of Foxdown Wood. Then he put the machine down. 'We'll start by interviewing them, and see if they fit your description. What sort of a car was it? Did you see?'

Cathy opened her mouth to say, 'No,' when she remembered that Vix had said something about it being red and shiny. But she couldn't tell them what make it was. Then she looked at the police radio and her face lit up.

'There is one thing...' She pulled her walkie-talkie out of her pocket. 'We had been going to play with these in the woods on Friday when Matt had to go back home. When Mum and I went looking for him early this morning I found this near where we were planning to go. There's a chance—a very slim chance—that he might still have the other one and his battery might still be holding out. He might even be trying to call me. This battery is almost dead though.'

The policeman looked at Cathy with new respect and turned the toy over in his hand. It looked silly and cheap next to his heavy-duty equipment. He picked up his radio and spoke into it. 'I think we have a useful bit of information here,' he said. 'I'm just popping back to the station with Ms Mackeson for some batteries. Would you have something to boost and trace a faint radio signal? Good. Then I think we might be in business.'

***

Harry Carter sat stiffly in the back of the police car, looking straight ahead. He barely nodded to Cathy as she got in next to him.

'I'm glad the police are here,' she volunteered at last, desperate to break the silence.

'Are you?' he snapped. 'I'm not. They'll think I don't do a good job of looking after Matt. Then, when they find him, they'll probably take him into care after this, I'll...' As he talked, Mr Carter's ears got redder and redder, and he clenched his fists.

Cathy just bit her lip and looked out of the window. Matt was right, his Dad's obsession with being the perfect parent was making him odd.

At least *her* Mum wasn't perfect. She was just good enough. For the first time ever, Cathy felt a warm glow of appreciation of Maggie's shortcomings. She wondered how her Mum was doing on her nursing mission in the Other World. Funny to think of her Mum, who was so nifty at putting stitches in, also swinging a lethal scimitar. Although she only *said* she was a warrior, Cathy had never seen her 'at it', so to speak.

At the police station, batteries were put into the little plastic walkie-talkie, its wavelength was calculated, and three police car radios were tuned into that frequency.

Everyone held their breath. Nothing.

'We won't pick up anything unless he has it turned on, of course, and we can't make contact with him,

114

either.' The sergeant looked worried. 'How long has he been missing? Since Friday evening? It's now,' he looked at his watch, 'Sunday 11.46 am. If I were in his shoes, I'd put it on for a few minutes every hour, and hope someone was listening. Once one or two of our cars have picked up a signal, we'll be able to pinpoint him... If his walkie-talkie is still working, of course.'

The police car stopped in a lay-by near the entrance to Longacre Lane. 'What if Matt is out of range?' Cathy did not like the thought; it scared her.

Midday came and went. All Cathy could think of was that she had not really eaten the day before because she had been unwell and, although she had nibbled some fruit and bread in Harawed's camp, she wasn't sure how long ago that was. Now she was very, very hungry. 12.05 pm, 12.15 pm. The car began to steam up and get uncomfortable. Cathy's tummy began to rumble very loudly.

At last, at 12.39 pm the sergeant handed Cathy a five-pound note. 'Go and get us all chips, love. This could be a long wait. Extra vinegar on mine.'

But hardly had Cathy stepped out of the car, when a faint crackling came over the radio. 'Cathy? Cathy? Are you there?' The voice sounded really miserable. There was more crackling which sounded like a loose connection, then nothing.

'He didn't give us a moment to answer!' Cathy moaned miserably. 'We missed him.'

Voices came thick and fast over the radio, giving bearings and directions. The sergeant pushed his microphone into Cathy's hand. 'It's only about a mile away. If he speaks again, you and his Dad keep him talking, see if you can get any clue as to where he might be.'

'But I thought you'd got a bearing?' Mr Carter sounded irritated.

'We have, but it's only rough. It was a very short transmission and the signal was very weak. We aren't 'Star Trek'—we can't beam him up. However, anything he can tell us will be of help. What he can see from the window, if there is one; if he can hear anything nearby, traffic, farm machinery, that sort of thing. Just get him to tell you everything.'

The car was speeding along the main road towards Walliford but, at a small industrial estate to the south, they suddenly turned left very sharply to park behind a line of tatty-looking garages. Cathy was told to stay in the car by the sergeant, but Mr Carter climbed out and stood with his hands next to the window. His knuckles were quite white, and his hands were shaking. Cathy could see no more of him than that. But it was enough to know that he was scared.

Mr Carter did love Matt. He just didn't know how to show it. Cathy felt sorry for him.

Just then, a clatter made her turn her head. One of the garage doors had been opened. Then another, and another. A police officer in a Day-Glo-yellow safety vest was fitting keys to the doors one by one, and flinging them wide. Mr Carter took a few hesitant steps forward, then he ran from garage to garage, calling frantically, 'Matt! Matt! Where are you?'

At the end of the row the sergeant and several officers stood together in a huddle and compared notes on the bearings. 'It was such a weak signal, sir, it could be anywhere in this estate. It stretches for quite a long way, all along behind these woods.'

'So he could be in the woods?' Mr Carter asked, horrified.

The sergeant turned and looked at the scrubby woods that came up to the edge of the road. 'I guess so, but not far from this spot. There are so many little workshops and garages around here, it's almost impossible to tell. We'll just have to call for reinforcements and dogs and search the lot.'

Just then, a short, sharp bark echoed in the woods to their left, and a small vixen hobbled through the undergrowth.

'Vix!' Cathy squealed, as she leaped out of the police car and ran across the scrub and rubbish to where she had seen her friend. She was so anxious she forgot that in this world the little fox would be a normal, terrified little animal. Cathy

Vix was gone, of course. The police sergeant came and quietly told her she ought to sit in the car, where it might be safer. 'Anything could happen, now. In fact, I ought to send you home. Your Mum will wonder where you are.'

'No she won't, I left a note. Anyway,' she looked up so she could look him in the eye, 'this is important. That fox is Matt's friend. She never leaves Foxdown Wood, she must sense something important here. Foxes are like dogs, after all—don't you think she can smell him? Perhaps she can even hear him.'

The sergeant looked at Cathy, then into the undergrowth. Every second counted, but while they were waiting for tracker dogs to come from the police kennels in Oxford, why not sit quietly and see what the animal did? The girl did have a point.

He gave his orders quietly, and everyone got back

into the cars, making as little noise as possible, leaving the doors slightly open so there would be no sudden noises of hinges or catches.

And there they sat, minute after tense minute, listening for the tiniest sound from the radio, or from the fox. Cathy found she was clutching the radio handset until the edges dug into her hands, and her fingers were hurting.

The dogs would be here soon—they mustn't frighten Vix away. She must know something, or she would never have left the safety of Foxdown Wood—and to come *here* of all places, she would have had to have risked the main road, deadly at the best of times.

'I'm just going to see if I can find her, she knows my smell, she might not be too frightened of me.'

Cathy slipped quietly out of the passenger seat and slowly edged around the garages to the next row, most of which were daubed with slogans and cartoons, and draped with rusting barbed wire.

And, crouching on the end garage, one that looked as if it had been engulfed by a tangled elder tree, was Vix. When she saw Cathy, she stood, stumbled on her weak forepaw, and gave a short bark. Then she turned and slunk away into the scrubby undergrowth.

Two police officers who had been standing just behind Cathy immediately ran to the overgrown garage.

There they called, listened, and heard a muffled voice.

Right at the back, tied up behind a pile of rubbish was Matt.

'Thank goodness,' he whispered. 'I'm famished!'

Rogation Sunday

'But what about your claustrophobia?' Cathy was amazed that Matt was not a quivering wreck.

Now that Matt had bathed and put on fresh clothes, he looked a little more human. He was seated at his kitchen table demolishing a whole box of chocolate cakes.

'Once I realized I could see the outside I was all right. I could tell what colour the sky was. I could smell the air. I was tied up and in a dreadful spot, but the outside *was there*. It wasn't like there was no hope, no way out. That's what always freaks me. But the second night was really cold, and of course it was quite dark again. I kept thinking I'd dreamed I'd seen daylight. I kept myself sane by trying to remember my times tables. I still get them wrong, even at my age!'

'But weren't you frightened they might want to kill you?' Cathy was all agog.

'No, I don't think so. I did think about it, of course, especially in the dark hours when I couldn't see any-thing, and could only hear the occasional car go past or a dog barking. But when they came to bring me my food, I pretended I was a halfwit and didn't understand anything. I though they might let me go if they reckoned I was dim.'

Cathy laughed. 'It didn't need much pretending then!'

Matt threw the paper case from his cake at her. 'I'll get you for that,' he promised. 'Thank goodness they didn't find the walkie-talkie though.'

'It was really your fox that found you,' his Dad said, warmly. 'I am buying that animal's feed from now on. Two tins a day if she likes. It's the least I can do.'

Matt looked up, grinning at the thought of an extra hour in bed every morning. 'Thanks!' he spluttered, his mouth disgustingly full of cup-cakes.

His Dad laughed. It lessened the severity in his thin, square features. He actually looked quite nice.

Cathy decided it was time she left. Her Mum had come back about an hour before, and had promised to tell her everything that had happened over a very special nut roast and stuffing. Cathy could smell the aroma wafting in from next door already. 'See you later,' she waved, but Matt and his Dad were so engrossed in discussing what they would do for Vix, and how they were going to look after her from now on, they didn't even notice.

It was mid-afternoon when Matt and his Dad knocked on Maggie's door. Mr Carter looked rather embarrassed. 'You may think what I am about to say a little strange, Mrs Mackeson, but Matt told me about the wood and how he was kidnapped for overhearing the men's discussions... Well, I feel evil threatening us all, not just Matt, but Knapsden and maybe a lot more as well if we allow the wood to be built on. It was said in the old days that there was a sort of a Guardian of the Wood. Not everyone gives credence to the old tales, but I have my reasons to believe.'

Mr Carter looked as if he expected a challenge at this point. He pulled himself up straight, clenched his fists by his side, and wore his old, severe expression again.

Maggie simply nodded and smiled gently. 'Oh, I do so agree. There are definitely special places in this world, where our reality touches other, perhaps even greater ones. I think it's what used to be called a "Beth-el" in the olden days.'

Mr Carter looked amazed at Maggie's response. He hesitated, then he replied rather hurriedly. 'I think I saw this "Guardian" once when my wife Ginny was dying. It looked like I'd imagine an angel to be.' Suddenly, he seemed embarrassed that he had let such an intimacy slip. He reddened and tried to explain away his confusion. 'I used to go to the woods a lot then. It was the only peace I could find, so I am sure you will appreciate I owe the wood something.'

Maggie stared at her hands, so she did not have to embarrass her neighbour by witnessing him blushing. She did not wish to compound his discomfort. 'I do know what you mean,' she said quietly.

He turned and looked out of the grimy kitchen window towards the edge of the wood that hung over the end of Maggie and Cathy's garden. 'Well,' he continued, finding his equilibrium at last, 'there's an old tradition that goes back, oh, many centuries. It happened around about Rogationtide, which is now. The farmer who owned the land around here would harness his two finest horses and plough the borders of the wood. It was said that as long as the edges of the wood were cared for, then evil would be kept out of the wood and the whole village—it was all done properly, with the correct Church of England prayers for the event, of course. Nothing suspect about it,' he added, anxiously.

Harry Carter looked very serious and intense, but underneath, he bubbled like an excited schoolboy... 'Well, I've been thinking. I've lived here all my life and I've only seen it done a couple of times. In fact, it's not been done since I was a small boy, but I'd like to do it now. I think I would feel we'd strengthened the wood by doing it and honoured the good, old ways.

'Although it looks as if the developers will be arrested and, if what Matt says is right, they may not even own all the land at all. But there is always the risk that someone else might take up the planning option. I want to fight for Foxdown Wood to be saved.'

This fighting talk appealed to Maggie. She was quite intrigued. 'Is this tradition like beating the bounds?' she asked.

'Yes, that used to happened as well, but it would need more organization that we can achieve this afternoon. Anyway, if you will come with me, I've borrowed two of the dray shires from the King William Brewery where I work. I've got Duke, a beautiful eighteen-hands dark bay gelding, and Duchess at sixteen-and-a-half, she's a light bay.'

Harry leaned back against the kitchen sink and looked exhausted. That was the longest and most revealing speech he had made in a long time. Suddenly, he stared at the floor, twisting his thin hands, wondering if his neighbours would think he was mentally deranged.

'I love old ceremonies and suchlike,' Maggie enthused. 'What do we do? Just walk round the wood with two horses. 'Would the farmer allow us to plough around the edges?'

Harry looked up, slightly surprised that Maggie had liked his idea. He shook his head. 'I doubt if we can do the ploughing—especially without notice. But it won't be just us; it needs the Vicar, of course, and she can be here after evening prayer, at 6 pm. We'll have our own proper little Rogation Sunday parade. The horses will have their blue and yellow flight ribbons in their manes and we will have to sing as loudly as we can. All we need now is people... Will you come?'

Maggie beamed with delight. 'Of course! What about you, Cathy?'

Cathy was about to pout and think of an excuse, when she saw Matt frantically nodding behind his Dad's shoulder. Then she saw the point. It was no pottier than going to a parallel world to help a strange, dark-eyed King with a plaited silver beard. It was fighting with what one had, even if it might only appear to be make-believe. If people believed it was an ancient way of keeping the wood and the village safe and, if it was done with the proper prayers and everything, perhaps it would have an effect in the other world. Perhaps it would send 'ripples' through to defeat Harawed. They had met with no success finding 'words of strength,' but at least this was something they *could* do.

'OK,' she said at last, 'when and where?'

***

The wood was filled with late afternoon sun when the small group met at the entrance to Longacre Lane. The rich smell of bluebells and early fungi growing was quite heady, and the young leaves, still pale before the summer sun darkened them, shimmered brilliantly against the browns and deep greens of the mossy trunks and branches. A pair of small, brown wrens were diving in and out of the undergrowth, with sprigs of dried grass in their beaks.

The two great shires had been dressed in a hurry by Matt and Harry, but their manes were neatly plaited and tied with bright blue and yellow ribbons. Cathy was nervous of the huge horses, but risked patting their bright, star-shaped blazes as they bowed and nodded for the Polo mints that Matt slipped them.

Cathy had never stroked a shire horse before, and jumped back when Duke snorted at her. She thought they looked magnificently handsome with their fine, white feathers brushed to perfection around their hooves. Suddenly, Duke made a dive for Cathy's shoulder, giving her a playful shove. Cathy screamed a little, but Matt just laughed. 'He thinks it's about time you dished up some goodies. Here,' he tossed her a packet of mints.

'Time to go,' announced the Vicar, a short, jolly-looking blonde lady called Betty. 'I've always wanted to do the Rogation prayers. It's supposed to be for blessing the seed that has been sown. But my old parish thought it was irrelevant and old-fashioned. Right, we're off!'

And with that the small procession started off around the wood. Longacre Lane was straight for most of the way, the wood on the left and the open, chalky fields on the right. Large knobs of chalk and flint lay strewn like dinosaur bones for as far as the eye could see. Then, after about a hundred metres, it turned left into the wood, leading them to where the developers had parked their car when they kidnapped Matt. After that, the lane narrowed into a track which passed between two stones, one upright and the other looking decidedly drunk and staggering.

'How odd!' Maggie whispered, as they passed between the stones. 'The track stops quite suddenly here, as if it forgot where it was going.'

Just then, Cathy, grabbed hold of Matt's sleeve, 'No, it didn't forget. Look!'

And the track was indeed going on, outside the wood now, skirting the edge for quite a long way. Cathy noticed that it was now dawn on a midsummer's day, not late afternoon in an English spring. They had all walked between the stones, right into the Other World, with the open downs spreading before them.

Cathy sneaked a sideways look at the others.

Matt was grinning widely as he tried to sing. Maggie was trying hard to keep going too, but it was as if the others had not seen where they were. The vicar did not stop her warbling, nor did Mr Carter and the solitary choirboy falter in their hymn-singing. As far as they knew, they were still in an English wood. Behind them slipped the small, russet shape of a limping fox.

Cathy and Matt kept singing as long as they could, but the sight of wild, red-headed warriors running towards them, brandishing huge broadswords, made them falter in their words.

Maggie hesitated for only a few seconds before unhitching Duchess from her harness and leaping up onto the great mare's wide back, with an agility that Cathy would not have believed possible in her old Mum. Then, tearing a dead branch from a tree, Maggie turned the animal's head towards the three dozen or so warriors running at breakneck speed towards them. At the sight of the small, dark-haired woman waving what looked for all the world like a scimitar, riding the biggest monster these people had ever seen, they dropped their weapons and ran for all they were worth.

Matt soon unhitched Duke, scrambled up his broad back and put down his hand to help Cathy up behind him. 'Quick, I think we've found some "magic"! These people have never seen horses before! Especially ones that come out of the woods!'

'Perhaps they think the horses are the ghosts from the wood they're so frightened of!' Cathy laughed as she scrambled awkwardly up behind Matt and held on to the back of his shirt very tightly. She had never ridden before and was amazed at her own coolness as she settled on the animal's great, wide back.

'Grip very hard with your knees,' Matt called, 'keep your back straight and hold tight to me. We're off!'

Suddenly her whole world lurched as Matt coaxed Duke away from the others in shade of the wood. The few of Harawed's men who had not fled at the sight of Maggie on Duchess, turned and ran as the second horse trotted amiably towards them. The huge warriors screamed and fled in sheer panic.

'Go back! Keep near the trees!' Maggie ordered. 'They are frightened of the Guardian of the Wood, as long as they think we are from him and under his protection, they will be terrified. If we go too far onto the open land we'll become just a monstrous curiosity.'

Matt pulled on Duke's bridle and turned him back to the main party, who had kept singing throughout. It seemed as if they were aware only of being in an English wood on a warm spring afternoon. The open chalk downs ahead and the warriors closing in all around simply did not exist. They just kept singing the beautiful and ancient words of a psalm as the late afternoon sun was streaming through the young leaves all around them.

A little way off, well into open ground, the warriors regained their composure and turned back to watch the great horses and their riders. Not one dared advance. They were no less terrified of the small group of small, oddly-dressed people singing lustily and slightly flat. These strange creatures had come out of the wood. The stories were true!

In terror and amazement they let their great hands hang loose as the procession walked steadily around the edges of the wood until the King's lodge was in sight. Matt cheered. The palisade and longhouse were burned and battered, but still standing.

'Now we will see whether these "words of strength" work or not!' Maggie declared, as she straightened her back and, taking a deep breath, called, 'Harawed, Methwin! The Guardian of the Wood demands you come to bring your case before him!'

The Guardian is Awake!

Tentatively, the gates of the Lodge swung open.

Maggie's challenge had been relayed by swift runners to both camps. Methwin responded so quickly, it was almost as if he had been ready and waiting. The king came out, attended by three of his warriors, all wearing their formal forest-green cloaks and carrying leafy branches as signs of peace.

Slowly, they made their way towards the edge of the wood where Maggie and the others had halted, still singing the old hymns, most of them quite oblivious to anything other than a little Rogationtide ramble in the woods.

From the downs beyond, where Harawed's pavilions stood, came a similar party—Harawed with his three warriors, one of whom was the huge, red-headed woman in heavy armour, who seemed to be his battle chief. These four were dressed in flame-red cloaks and were empty-handed.

'A bad sign,' muttered Maggie. 'The fact they have come means they are willing to talk, but they're bound to have swords under their cloaks. In this land, if you are carrying something that grows it means you are committed to peace.'

'But you were fighting with a stick just now, Mum,' Cathy argued.

'Yes, only to defend myself. I *am* committed to peace. That's why I've challenged them both to come forward to be judged by the Guardian. Real battles are terrible and rarely solve anything.'

Matt leaned across from his great height on Duke's back, whispering in case anyone else should hear: 'But what if nothing happens?'

Maggie just grinned and she urged Duchess forward a little. 'Let's just see, shall we?'

As the parties approached, Maggie turned Duchess and rode calmly but steadily back towards the edge of the wood, where the knoll stood tall and proud. Cathy realized with astonishment that the steep little rise behind her was very different from the hazel-coppiced mound she knew so well. Here, the slopes were bare, with an open view all the way from east to west and only one solitary hazel tree at the top. The two woods were not quite the same, it seemed.

Maggie dismounted and beckoned the children to do the same. 'We mustn't be seen to be trying to hide behind monsters,' she told them. 'This is between the Guardian and them. We must do nothing that could be construed as trying to weight things either way.'

'Do you think there really is something in the wood?' Cathy looked very worried as she glanced back over her shoulder.

'Yes, I do. Whether it's an angel as Harry Carter thinks, or something else, I'm not sure. But whoever is here, it's up to her or him now.' Maggie's face was set with a firm expression as she watched the two parties coming nearer and nearer.

Cathy wasn't so calm. 'But why did you make the challenge? What if it all goes horribly wrong? I'm scared!'

Maggie shrugged. 'I haven't the foggiest what's going to happen. Methwin taught me that the knoll is an ancient meeting place between the people and the Guardian of the Wood. I know Kings and Queens are always made here, so challenging both sides to let the Guardian choose just seemed the right thing to say.'

Maggie stepped forward, drawing herself up to her full height as the two parties arrived. She looked so small next to the great giants, their wide red and green cloaks billowing like great sails in the breeze. In her arms, Maggie still carried the curved, scimitar-like branch she had pulled from a tree earlier. She held it like a sceptre, and looked every inch a King's daughter. Most important of all, she looked quite calm, and as if she knew exactly what she was doing.

Cathy admired that and she tried to put a similar look on her own face. Then Matt nudged her and asked if she felt OK, or was she going to be sick, so she stopped.

Harawed and Methwin were standing opposite each other, with Maggie in the middle. Vix, who had kept fairly out of sight so far, slunk between them and crouched at Maggie's feet.

Harawed was the first to speak. Bowing in mock reverence to Maggie he said, 'I see you have to ride monsters to be great enough to look me in the eye,' he sneered. 'You are not to be trusted. You did not come back to see me as you promised.'

'Yes I did. I am here now, aren't I?' Maggie retorted.

Methwin stepped next to his adoptive daughter and pointed into the depths of the wood. 'Take heed, boy, the Guardian is awake. We have been called to put our cases before him and to see whose claim is just. There will be no escape for you if you do not leave now. So give up your unjust claim to this land and the throne that belongs to its own people.'

Harawed jerked a thumb towards the little group of Rogation singers. 'And is this the biggest army you could raise against me? Two beasts, which I assume from legend are horses, a lame fox, together with a fat lady, a boy and a skinny man!' Harawed put in hand on his heart on mock fear. 'Even you, Uncle, must have been able to put together a show a little more impressive than this!'

Maggie did not hesitate, she walked up to Harawed and looked him in the eye. 'Go on then, up to the Sacred Knoll if you're not scared. Call the Guardian to meet you face to face and crown you, if he will. Go then, or will you let your warriors see you are frightened of a legend?'

Harawed flushed deep crimson under his tanned skin. But he did not hesitate. He knew his warriors had gathered behind him, slowly edging closer and closer, eager to miss nothing. Harawed knew they must not see the slightest flinch. Anyway, what was there to fear? There was no bright Guardian of their world. The wood was just a wood. There were simply a few special places in the fabric of the Universe, where, as the Lady

131

Margaret had explained to him once, people and these 'horse' things could stray through from other worlds. Her world in particular.

As Harawed passed Duke, he prodded the animal, intrigued to feel the great muscles as steady and strong as his own. He ran a hand over the proud strong neck, and tugged at the blue and yellow ribbons to see if they were part of the horse's hair or not.

He nodded his approval. 'It's a good beast,' he muttered to himself, as he climbed to the top of the mound in a few strides. 'I could do with him. I will take him when his charade is over. He could carry me easily, making me taller and swifter of foot than anyone else in this land... Then they would *have* to see that I am King.'

Finally, he stood at the top and turned round. He pulled his crimson turban loose, so his hair streamed long and black over his shoulders. He flung his great vermilion cloak wide so it flapped like an enormous, regal bird in the wind. He stood, huge, magnificent, handsome and totally unafraid. With his right hand he reached to his side and unsheathed a sword almost as long as himself, with a gloriously wrought gold hilt. The weapon flashed in the sun as he swung it high. The tip reached almost to the top of the small hazel tree. Harawed smiled, showing his strong, white teeth. He knew the effect he was creating.

The crowds that had gathered at a respectful distance from the wood gasped at the sight. Maggie took a sideways glance at Methwin. He was still tall and commanding, but his hair was very white, and frailty was beginning to tell in his limbs.

Matt and Cathy could see that something would

have to be done to establish this land's peace and justice. But what? At this moment Harawed had everything completely in his hands.

The crowd was closing in tightly on all sides, men and women dressed in Methwin's green and Harawed's red. As the crowd gathered, the warriors all thronged together, waiting to see whether Harawed would complete the ancient tradition of asking the Guardian to give him the crown.

Cathy looked around, amazed at the size of the crowd that had silently gathered. She leaned over and whispered into Matt's ear, 'Who's fighting whom? Who are the goodies and who are the baddies?'

'Search me. I guess they're all much the same. Perhaps some good guys were bullied and blackmailed into fighting for Harawed, and some shady characters are fighting for Methwin. Who can tell? Frightening though, isn't it?'

Just then, Harawed began to speak.

'Hear me, people. Hear me, Guardian of this place. Methwin is old and frail, and weak in the mind. I, Harawed, nephew of the sometime King, do claim my rightful place as King in his stead.'

The Fall of Harawed

Harawed swept the point of his sword over the awestruck upturned faces below him. 'You do not challenge me?' he bellowed. Then he turned his back on the crowd and swung the blade towards the wood. 'And you, *ancient Guardian*,' he roared sarcastically, 'what is your challenge?' And he gave his sword an extra flourish as he turned back to face the crowd.

It was at that second when Harawed was slightly off balance that Vix decided to leap. She didn't leap *at* Harawed exactly, but at something just beyond him, something that nobody saw. In the split second before she moved, Matt saw Vix pull back her ears, bare her teeth and raise her hackles. He was about to ask her what the matter was when she sprang, jumping so close to Harawed that he stumbled and fell. The crowd of watching warriors went berserk. 'The Guardian has spoken, Harawed has fallen. He is not fit to lead us— we will be guided by Methwin!

But as they rushed towards Harawed, running and leaping up the knoll, determined to kill him as ruthlessly as he had killed others, the fallen giant raised his broadsword. Its exquisite gold workmanship gleamed in the bright sun...

There was a flash of lightning...

And he was no longer there!... Neither was Vix.

Suddenly there was a loud CRACK! and a burning smell, and the body of Vix reappeared, rolling back down the slope to lie at the feet of Duke. Matt ran over to her and stroked the soft, warm muzzle of his beloved fox as the blood oozed from her, wasting her life on the earth.

Reverend Betty, the choirboy and Harry Carter all stopped singing. They looked down at Matt, who was cradling the body of his best friend in his arms. 'What happened?' Betty demanded. 'Who did that?'

A quick glance around showed Maggie that they were back in England, and the lingering smell of gunpowder told her that someone with a gun was near.

Flinging her stick aside, Maggie began to rip at the lining of her padded jacket, making an impromptu bandage for the poor fox.

Matt began sobbing. His Dad would think he was soft, but he didn't care. He let his tears fall freely. He was not ashamed of loving Vix. With trembling hands he stroked and comforted the limp animal, as she gazed up in utter bewilderment at her Boy. She was too wounded to struggle or bite as Maggie bound the rags around the animal's quivering flanks.

Then, making a stretcher out of hazel branches and the vicar's surplice, Matt and his Dad carried Vix very gently towards the lane.

'I can't imagine how we got so deep into the wood with the horses,' said Reverend Betty, looking around, amazed. 'I was sure we were only keeping to the boundaries. But it did seem to be a very *peculiar* place, I kept thinking I saw all sorts of funny things—strange warriors waving swords and so on! Whatever next! But it was probably the cheese I had for lunch giving me indigestion.'

'I expect we all ran further into the wood when we heard the shot,' Mr Carter assured her. 'It all happened so quickly that we did not notice where we were, that's all. When we get to the lane, would you be so kind as to take take my son into Walliford, to the vet? Do you know where he is? I'll have to take the horses back to the brewery. Oh dear, Mrs Mackeson. It looks as if our plan did not work. We haven't kept evil out of the wood, it seems.'

Maggie shrugged. 'You can never tell how things will work out. But I'm going to call the police as soon as I get back, I don't like this firing guns in the wood, especially when there're children and animals around.'

'I'd like a word with them as well,' Mr Carter added. 'I want to know how they're getting on trying to find Matt's captors.'

Vix was placed in the back of Reverend Betty's estate car, amid a jumble of wellington boots and gardening tools. Matt spent the whole journey leaning over the back seat and stroking Vix's warm, wiry hair, talking very quietly to her as her small rib cage rose and fell, shuddered and heaved again.

She seemed so warm, and so alive as she fought for each breath, that when her little body suddenly lay quite still, Matt started in disbelief.

Suddenly he screamed, '*NO!*' so loudly that the vicar swerved, narrowly missing a lorry.

She pulled over onto a grass verge and got out to open the boot.

The fox was dead and Matt's tousled red hair was buried in his grimy arms. Reverend Betty stood watching for a few seconds, then very quietly she shut the boot and turned the car around. 'We'll go home now,' she said quietly.

Matt was as white as a sheet as he picked up the limp, warm little animal and carried her into the shed.

'I'll hold a funeral service for her after school tomorrow, if you like,' the vicar offered. 'I can be here just after 4.30 pm.'

Matt wanted to show his appreciation, but his eyes, head and throat hurt too much with trying not to cry. He just swallowed and nodded. 'Thanks. I'll bury her on the knoll,' he muttered and ran inside.

The police had arrived by the time Harry Carter had finished putting the horses back into their stables. He had come home irritated because Duke had lost some of the yellow and blue flight ribbons that had been tied to the proudly plaited mane.

Matt was huddled in a heap on the settee when his Dad showed the sergeant in. It was the same man who had helped to rescue Matt earlier in the day. 'I'm surprised to see you up, Matt. I would have thought you would have gone to bed for the day after your ordeal.'

Matt shrugged, but didn't look up. 'I had one or two things I really wanted to do. But I'm tired now, and I'm feeling very angry. My fox died, you know. She didn't even make it to the vet. I'd like to shoot whoever shot her! I'm off to bed now if no one needs me.' He hauled himself upright and turned to go upstairs.

'Before you go, did you see anything of the person who shot your fox?' the sergeant asked kindly.

Matt shook his head miserably. 'The first I knew was a bang and the smell of singed fur and gunpower.'

The sergeant stood up. 'Well, if no one actually saw anyone holding a gun, there is nothing we can do until we have more information. I'll be on my way. We'll keep you informed if we discover anything, of course.'

'And what about my son's kidnappers?' Mr Carter interjected. 'We haven't had much information about *them* lately. What are you *doing* exactly?' Matt's Dad had drawn himself up to his full height, and had resumed the tight, closed look he always used to wear.

The policeman tried to look reassuring. 'We haven't got any further on that, I'm afraid. The men who own the wood, a Mr French and his son, are not at home. The neighbours don't know where they are, but they do answer the description that Cathy Mackeson gave when she told us about the men she overheard planning to build shoddy houses and leave the country.'

'Well, we all guessed that much,' Harry Carter snapped, leaning on the table and staring the policeman right in the eye. 'When are you going to start doing some proper, thorough police work and get them captured? They could be out of the country by now for all we know! And I want to know if my son is safe to walk the streets. He does a newspaper round in the mornings, you know!'

'We *are* doing proper police work, Mr Carter. The Frenchs' house is being watched. We'll know the second they return. I am sure that Matt is safe, as long he does not go wandering in the woods on his own, and tries to be sensible. I would suggest that he does not do his paper round until we're certain we have his abductors.'

'Thank goodness, a lie in,' Matt sighed, as he closed the door to the cupboard-like staircase and went upstairs.

'I'm not sure that *is* a proper, thorough job. They're still loose, aren't they?' Harry Carter scowled heavily as he showed the sergeant to the door.

***

After school, Cathy went to Matt's house. Mr Carter had let Matt off school, ostensibly to catch up on sleep, but Matt had used the time to slip out and dig a deep grave for Vix at the spot on the Knoll where she used to sit and wait for her Boy to come and feed her. He did not think the kidnappers would come back. He did not care if they did. Vix deserved a decent funeral, and men like them weren't going to stand in his way. The digging had been hard, but he had given himself a rest, intending to do some more before Reverend Betty turned up.

He guessed that his conventional Dad would be most upset at the thought of a funeral service for an animal, so he said nothing, but slipped out of the house to make his preparations alone.

Just as Cathy came home from school, two police officers turned up at Matt's door.

'Mr Nicholas French and his son Harley, the developers of Foxdown Wood, were arrested a few minutes ago as they arrived at their home in Streeting. In the back of the car was a recently-fired shotgun, which probably killed Matt's fox and for which they did not hold a licence. The men answer the description of the kidnappers, and have been charged with the offence. The shooting in a manner which is likely to cause harm is another little gem the magistrates will enjoy hearing about. The conversations you and Cathy overheard about the men's plans for the wood are also being investigated. We will let you know when the trial will be and we are not recommending bail.'

The sergeant seemed pleased with himself, but Matt was too miserable to be glad.

'I know just what Dad will say, "Well at least you seem to have done *something* properly at last!"' he mimicked.

The policeman winced visibly. 'I think I'll send my colleague here to his place of work to inform him. I've got... er... other things to attend to. Cheerio, I'm glad everything seems to be working out OK!'

'That's not what I'd call it,' Matt replied miserably, as he lifted the stiff, cold shape in a bin bag onto his shoulder.

He refused Cathy's help to carry Vix. She was *his* fox, and he would carry her all the way to her grave.

He wanted to cry again, but decided to wait until later when he was on his own. Cathy felt for him, and did not quite know whether to talk or be silent.

'My Mum says that even though the two Mr Frenchs have been arrested, the planning permission on this land still stands. It's only a matter of time before the bulldozers move in and flatten the wood for some other owner.' Cathy was panting to keep up with Matt, although Vix's body was far heavier than the spade she was carrying. Despite this, he was still way ahead of her, negotiating the wood as if he, too, were a fox.

He only grunted in reply.

Cathy tried to catch her breath. Then she called out again. 'But don't you see, this will threaten Methwin's world again, as well as our wood? It's far from all over.'

Matt still only grunted and glowered at her. 'So what? Now Vix is dead, there's nothing to keep the wood here for! They can flatten it for all I care. There is no Other World anyway, I thought you knew it was all pretend. It's just a kids' game to take away the pain of death and reality. You don't know what it's like having someone you love dying!'

'Oh yes I do—my Dad.'

'But he's alive. You can still see him.'

'But we're not together anymore. It feels like he's dead.'

'But he is still alive!'

'That only makes it worse. Knowing he's still alive and I can't see him every day. Everyone is as fit as a flea, but I can't have my family back like it used to be. You can't imagine what it feels like!'

Matt did not reply, he marched on, the heavy black sack swinging from his shoulder.

Cathy felt her face burning with anger and embarrassment. So he thought she was just a kid playing games, and that his problems were worse than her own. Well she'd show him. She flung the shovel down and started to run back. He could bury Vix by himself, and if the bulldozers dug her up again, well, why should she care?

Just then she heard Matt shouting, 'Cathy! Cathy! Come here!'

She kept walking in the direction of her home. Why should she do what he said? After all, he was just a rude, insensitive boy. Why had she bothered to be friendly with him? Anyone capable of putting frogs and chewing-gum in her lunch-box really wasn't worth the effort. She should have realized that at the beginning.

'Cathy! *CATHY!*' Matt persisted, running and crashing through the undergrowth as fast as he could towards her. She stopped and turned, giving him her most supercilious smile. 'Yes?' she inquired sweetly. 'Can I help you?'

He tugged at her arm and pulled. 'Come quickly, I've found something! Come on!'

Despite her anger, she followed. 'What is it?'

'I don't know, but it could save the wood.'

She shook her arms free of his grip. 'Let go of me! I thought you didn't care about the wood any more!'

'Look, I'm sorry, OK? I was upset, come on, do, please!'

Cathy shrugged and followed sluggishly as Matt bounded ahead.

Through the trees she could see a short, round figure bending over something on the ground. Reverend Betty had arrived ahead of them. She stood up and beamed at Cathy as she approached. 'Guess what we've found?'

'I don't know unless you tell me!' Cathy did not feel like being co-operative. It was all too much effort. Her head was aching with too many painful memories and thoughts. 'What did anything matter? No one understood what she had been through, or what she felt about anything. She didn't care about the wood. Why had she let herself dream about other worlds? Matt was right. It was all pretend, trying to cheer herself up in her head.

It was all eyewash. She was so angry with herself, with the rest of the world. With everything.

But what was lying on the ground between Betty and Matt made Cathy forget her anger completely.

THE FIND

20

Reverend Betty was busy polishing something with a handkerchief. In her hand was the unmistakable gleam of gold. There was no sign of corrosion; the metal was quite pure.

Cathy forgot all her woes and whistled quietly. 'Wow! Where did you find that?... What is it, anyway?'

The vicar wrapped the piece in the edge of her cassock and lifted it up. 'To me, it looks like an ancient sword hilt. Look, here's where the blade has snapped off. But there's only one way to tell for sure—we must take it to the Castle Museum at Walliford. If it really is valuable, we may have saved the wood.'

'But how?' Cathy was bemused.

'Simple!' Matt grinned. 'If this is ancient, the wood might be declared a site of special historical interest or something, and the planning permission could be withdrawn.'

Cathy looked down at the hole dug for Vix's grave. 'Did you find it in there?' she jerked her thumb downwards.

'Yes, I was just trying to make it a bit deeper so... well, so other animals wouldn't dig her up. Then the spade hit metal, and that was it.' Suddenly he peered closer at his find in dismay, rubbing at his with his dirty fingers. 'I say, I hope I haven't dented it or anything.'

'No. It looks as good as new, in fact. We'll have to dig another grave to bury Vix. You can't put her there, because archaeologists will want to examine the area.'

Matt hadn't thought of that. In the excitement, he'd forgotten why they were digging there at all. 'I'll open up her earth a bit, then she can lie where she always slept. She'd like that.'

Reverend Betty looked at her watch, 'I hate to rush you folks, but I've got to get back soon. Do you think it would be OK if we said the prayers first and you buried her afterwards?'

'Yes,' Matt said miserably. 'That'll be fine.' What did it matter anyway? Vix was dead, and, although he now had Cathy as a friend, he used to tell Vix things that he wouldn't have whispered to another living soul.

Reverend Betty dusted the mud off her cassock and started to read a passage from the Bible about heaven being full of animals: lions and lambs, even bears and wolves. 'I'm sure the good Lord will let foxes in as well,' she smiled. Then she finished with a prayer asking God to comfort Matt and Cathy.

After a few minutes' silence, the vicar gently closed her little book, shook Matt's hand, gave Cathy a hug and a kiss and turned to go. 'I'll see you soon. Ring me and let me know how you get on at Walliford Castle Museum.'

Silent, and still stunned from both the brilliant and awful things which had seemed to be happening all at the same time, Matt picked up the spade and dug at Vix's earth until it opened wide. Then he carefully slipped the black plastic bag, with the cold, stiff little body, deep down inside. They had some discussion as to whether they should take Vix out of the bag first, but they both liked the idea of keeping the rain and cold off her. Then Matt made a hole near her head 'So she can see the light and won't be scared,' he said quietly, and Cathy knew what he meant.

She carefully dug some bluebell corms and buried them deep into the soft soil above the earth. Both of them were crying by this time, but they shared a tissue and remarked that it was early for them to be getting hay fever.

The next day, after school, Matt and Cathy went Walliford Castle Museum with Maggie. The curator was quite intrigued by their find. It was indeed a broadsword hilt, she said, very old, but not Celtic or any other workmanship she recognized, possibly an import from Persia or somewhere. She telephoned the county coroner there and then, as the piece was probably Treasure Trove. 'If it is declared Treasure Trove it'll have to go the British Museum for photographing and dating. There'll have to be an inquest, of course, but that shouldn't take long.'

'But why an inquest?' Cathy asked. 'I thought that was for murders and stuff?'

'It is, normally, but the coroner has to establish where this was found and who owns it. Where did you find it by the way?'

'In Foxdown Wood,' Cathy answered. 'The land is owned by two scoundrels who are probably going to prison. It's not fair!'

Matt suddenly perked up, 'No, they don't own it! And especially not that bit of it! The sale of the main part of the Wood was supposed to go through today, but if they're in prison, they won't be able to sign anything, so the sale might not happen. And, even better, Vix's earth was on the strip between the knoll and Longacre Lane, and that belongs to the farmer who owns the land at the end of our garden! I was kidnapped for overhearing that, remember?'

'Then it depends on what the coroner decides, but the farmer and you two may own this between you!... unless you get prosecuted for trespassing, of course. Did you have permission to be digging on his land?'

'Ooops!' Matt and Cathy looked at each other in horror.

'Don't worry about that now, he may be so pleased to be offered a great deal of money for this sword hilt that he'll forgive you.'

'Cor, is it worth lots?' Matt's eyes were wide with delight.

'I believe so,' the curator replied, smiling. 'But there is one more phone call I must make—to the council offices, requesting a suspension of planning permission on Foxdown Wood until we've had a chance to look at the area properly.'

Solid Gold

21

A month later, Matt and Cathy came home from school to find they each had a large brown envelope post-marked London.

Both the envelopes contained a full report on the sword hilt and a beautiful set of full-colour photographs of the piece. The report said that the workmanship was of an unknown but very sophisticated people, and was of a quality that would have only belonged to royalty. Furthermore, it must have been wielded by someone at least two metres high, almost a giant in fact. This begged the vital question of how some ancient, hitherto undiscovered, culture could possibly have come as far as the Chilterns without any other known examples of their work being discovered. Analysis of the small remaining portion of the sword blade showed that, although it was made of something similar to iron, it also contained unrecognized elements and was quite uncorroded. The good state of the blade's metal seemed to suggest that the hilt could not have lain there long, although the expert who examined the piece was convinced that it might be as old as a thousand years.

The letter went on to say that this was all so strange and exciting that the wood was due to be carefully excavated in the near future, and may even be scheduled as an ancient monument.

'But archaeology is never clear cut,' the report ended. 'We have requested that the Department of the Environment permanently revoke the planning permission on the wood and schedule the area as an ancient monument of outstanding historical and scientific value, as the area holds clues to so much completely new information. We hope that the development of Foxdown Wood will not be allowed.'

Matt took his envelope round to Cathy. She and Maggie were just finishing reading the report when he came in. 'Well, would you believe it, the wood must have a Guardian after all!'

Maggie grinned as she poured tea. 'You bet. Dare I say, "I told you so"? Anyway, I have heard the planning permission is probably going to be revoked on the grounds that it was granted on false documentation in the first place. *And* I've heard that the farmer who owns the knoll is going to buy the rest of the wood as he always loved the place. So now it really is safe.'

'But do you think the Other World is safe too?' Cathy asked, then immediately felt silly for having asked it.

Matt flapped the envelope under Cathy's face. 'Of course it's safe. Harawed must have stumbled into this world, and I bet he couldn't get back again! He's probably in Walliford police station at this very moment, being charged as an illegal immigrant!'

Cathy shivered. 'I don't like the idea of him being

loose around here.'

Maggie put mugs of tea on the table. 'Well, they'll be digging like crazy to see what else they can find around there. Perhaps they'll unearth some clue as to what happened to him. But I have my own theory. Often, when I was a child and travelled between Methwin's world and home, I glimpsed, or thought I glimpsed, other places that I never went to. I think he might have slipped between these worlds, but dropped his sword in this one.'

'And landed somewhere else?' Cathy finished for her.

'And perhaps he landed nowhere—perhaps he just slithered through and missed.' Maggie added, in a matter of fact way.

'Ugh, what an awful thought!' Matt looked quite pale, as he did when his claustrophobia was getting him.

Maggie saw it, and added quickly, 'But wherever he is, the Guardian will keep him far away from us.'

Cathy looked confused. 'Do you think the walking the horses round the edge of the wood worked, then?'

'Don't you?' Maggie seemed to think it was obvious. 'Walking horses may or may not actually *do* anything, but to the people of Methwin's world it was a sign that their Guardian was still very much with them. People need a little faith, hope, and perhaps a dab of love to keep their hearts up.'

'But it wasn't their Guardian, it was *us*!' Cathy replied, feeling annoyed. She would have liked a story to be real and with a happy ending for once.

Maggie smiled and shook her head. 'But if the Wood had no Guardian, protecting the way between

Methwin's World and our own, we wouldn't have got there in the first place! He was very much a part of it all along.'

'But what about the "Words of Strength?"' Matt queried. 'That bit never happened.'

'But we were using words in the hymns we were singing, would that have been it?'

'It could well have been. But there could have been other words we were unaware of—words that the Guardian uttered which we didn't hear because they weren't for us. We don't actually *speak* Methwin's language after all, we only sort of *feel* it. Who knows? But something worked, whatever it was. But how it happened I guess we'll never really know.' Maggie replied.

Matt could see the point. 'It certainly seemed to give people the heart to stand up to a seriously dangerous bully.'

'Wherever he is.' Cathy shuddered.

Maggie patted Cathy on the back. 'He's not here, my pet. And if he was, he could do no harm. This is not his world. He'd have no power over us even if he was here.'

'Anyway,' she added brightly, 'I have some more news. I have a letter from Daddy here. He says he's sold our old house for a good price. He's sending me half the money and with his half he's buying a cottage just outside Norwich. You'll be able to go and stay with him whenever you like.'

Cathy did not respond.

'Aren't you pleased?'

'Where are *we* going to live then?'

'Where would you like to be?'

151

'I'd like to stay here at Foxdown Wood. Knighthayes Cottage is really cosy and nice now. I'd like to go and see Dad too, of course. My counsellor says I mustn't be scared of being angry with Dad, and going to see him to talk things through with him would be good. I'd like to go, but I'd like to live here as well.'

Maggie grinned. 'Good! Because Linda has offered to sell me the cottage very reasonably, and if the farmer does decide to share the money from the sale of the sword hilt with Matt and you, we could have central heating put in as well!'

'And my broken window mended?'

'We'll do that first, as long as Matt doesn't need to use it any more?'

Matt shook his head. 'No, it's too dangerous with your dustbin left in the way like that. I almost broke my neck! And, as well as that,' Matt added cheerfully, 'Dad and I have been talking for the first time, and he sees I need a bit more freedom now I'm older. I don't think I'll need to sneak out again.'

Then he looked oddly at Cathy. 'You go to a counsellor?'

'Yes, he's OK. I've had a couple of sessions, and I feel I'm beginning to come to terms with Mum and Dad's divorce. Although I don't think I'll ever really understand, at least I feel a bit more comfortable with things now.'

Matt looked rather worried. 'The police said I ought to have counselling when I came out of the garage place. I was a lot more shaken than I let on at the time. I'd like to talk to someone about it—about lots of things really: Mum dying, Dad's attitude about every-thing being perfect (he still washes the skirting-boards every week, it makes me scream!). But when I try and suggest I go to see someone, Dad gets mad and says that's only for nutters.'

'It's not that odd to want to talk to someone about stuff that bugs you, is it?' Cathy reasoned. 'It's really quite a normal thing to do, after all.'

'You're probably right. I used to tell Vix everything...' he added sadly. 'I'll think about it. Anyway,' he stood up, 'changing the subject, I'd like to go up to Vix's grave. Dad's given me some wood anemones to plant. D'you want to come, Cath?'

'Yes, I would, and I'd like to see if we can get back to Methwin's land as well. I want to know if everything's all right there.'

Maggie shook her head as she handed out chocolate biscuits for the journey. 'Don't be surprised if you can't get there,' she warned.

'Why ever not?' Cathy scowled. She still felt uncomfortable that her mother knew at least as much about the Other World as she did.

'Because it's the sort of place you go to when you are needed, or you need to go there yourself. It's not just like visiting a friend. You can't go just when you feel like it.'

'Well, I need to know what happened. I really do.'

'Me too,' muttered Matt through an extremely large mouthful of biscuit.

'Don't be surprised!' Maggie warned.

Harawed Again

The wood seemed to be overflowing with police and officials. A team of archaeologists from the university had dug two wide trenches between the trees, and a third, square pit around Vix's first grave where the wonderful sword hilt had been found.

'Sorry, you two, you can't come any closer.' A tall policeman they had not met before was standing firmly in their path. Behind him the square pit was cordoned off with wide, luminous yellow police 'no entry' tape. A tarpaulin had been strung tightly across the area, catching on the hazel branches as the wind blew.

'What on earth is going on here?' Matt asked. 'Can we at least know? We were the ones who discovered a sword hilt here.'

The sergeant who had found Matt came up to see what was happening. 'Ah, you two. Yes, I can tell you. The archaeologists have found an extraordinary skeleton, would you like to come and see?'

'No thanks!' Cathy grimaced.

'Yes please!' enthused Matt, but as the police tape was lowered so Matt could step over, Cathy suddenly found she had more curiosity than revulsion and jumped over the tape as well.

The pit was about half a metre deeper than Matt had dug. Everything was meticulously cut, marked and sectioned with tapes, flags and markers, until it looked more like a mathematical exercise than a hole in the ground.

At the bottom was a partially uncovered skeleton, huge and chalk-white, face down in the earth. The right hand was outstretched, fingers splayed wide and the left hand was curled close to the ribs as if it held a secret. The back of the skull was stained as black as charcoal, almost as if someone had dropped an ink bottle on it.

The sergeant stood looking down at the find with his arms crossed. 'The archaeologists reckon that, from the way the arm is stretched, he had been holding the sword you found, and dropped it as he stumbled forward. It looks like when he fell the sword was plunged into the ground, snapping it and leaving the handle loose, just as you found it. The rest of the blade was found rammed into the soil below the position of the hilt.'

'Wow, I wonder what killed him?' Matt enthused.

'The pathologist is just finishing. I expect he'll come and talk to you, as foul play isn't in question.'

'You mean he wasn't done in?' Matt was warming to his subject now.

'Well, what I mean is that he died a long time ago, so we won't be after whoever did it. But the interesting thing is that he was probably a prince or a king, judging by the golden rings and arm bands he was wearing. Furthermore he was a mighty big fellow. We can tell that for sure. He must have been about two metres tall, a giant by today's standards!'

Matt and Cathy looked at each other. 'Harawed!' they both exclaimed.

'What?' the police sergeant looked at them curiously.

'Nothing, just—a legend in these parts,' Matt replied, 'about a fighting giant. It's a very old tale.'

'And so is this chap,' chipped in a man with a white coat, plastic surgeon's gloves and an official-looking name tag that declared he was a police pathologist. 'The inquest will be open-and-shut. I'd say he's been lying here for the best part of a thousand years. By the burns on his skull, it looks as if he was struck on the head by lightning. It's what they used to call "an act of God" in the old days. A pretty painful way to go, but quick.'

'A thousand years! But the museum said the sword hadn't lain there long, although the hilt was probably very old!' gasped Cathy.

'That's right. That's why we were called in. We normally wouldn't bother to come and look at a chap as old as this one, but the fact that the sword fell there so recently, coupled with these...' The pathologist popped some little brightly-coloured objects into a small, plastic envelope and peeled off his gloves, 'made the archaeologists very curious indeed!'

'Can we look?' asked Matt, who thought the colours looked familiar.

The man held up the envelope, but the leaf mould clung to the untidy tangle of colours inside. 'These are the oddest thing of all. The dead man had them grasped in his left hand. There is no way they could have been put there recently although they look quite fresh and almost new. Yet he must have died with them in his fist.' He tapped the little plastic envelope to settle some of the clinging bits of earth and leaf mould, so they could see the contents more clearly. 'I'd love to take it back to the lab to do some tests, but the lot from the university are quite determined not to let anything out of their sight. What I call scientific analysis they call wandering about with finds! As we're not pressing any charges I'll not get a chance to investigate any further. Shame!'

'But what are they?' Cathy was intrigued.

Holding the bag in his palm, the pathologist shook his head in absolute bewilderment. 'I'd swear on oath these were scraps of modern blue and yellow nylon ribbon, cheap stuff at that, but there is no way anything even remotely like this existed until the beginning of the twentieth century. But I've learned never to be surprised in this job. The longer I work at it the more I'm convinced that absolutely anything is possible, and nothing is ever quite what it seems.'

Matt and Cathy exchanged glances. They knew exactly where the huge man had found modern ribbon. But there was no point in telling the police, or even the archaeologists. It would not make sense to any of them.

'Talking of anything being possible,' Matt said, remembering that they had been on their way to see Methwin, 'we've got places to go.'

'See you around,' the sergeant waved. 'Look in the paper next week and you'll get all the latest on what we've found.'

'You bet!' the children called, as they ran off in the direction of the tree-root tunnel. As they slithered down into the dip and pointed their feet at what had been their entrance into the Other World, they both hesitated and looked at each other.

For a few moments, neither of them dared say what they felt. 'What if we can't get through?' Matt ventured at last. 'What if we needed Vix to open the way?'

'Mum and I got through without her at least once. She said you have to need to go or to be needed there. I think it was more to do with the Guardian than Vix.'

There was a long pause.

'What if it was all a dream?' Cathy ventured.

'It wasn't. The ribbons prove that quite scientifically.'

Cathy hung her head and looked at the chalky hollow and the little dark tunnel under the great tree roots. Suddenly she pulled back her feet and hugged her knees. 'I'm not going,' she said decisively.

Matt looked at her, amazed. 'Scared you won't be able to get through this time? I am.'

'No... It's just that... well, I don't feel that what happened next in the Other World is anything to do with me at the moment. Maybe, like Mum, I'll go back one day to do something different. But not today. There's just some things in life you can't go back to. Even things you've loved. Things change and you just have to go on. But it's not such a bad thing all the time. Just think, we were sworn enemies a month ago, but I've discovered you're almost worth talking to!'

Matt squinted at her with a wry look. 'Yeah,' he said at last. 'You have your uses. Your Mum makes good cakes, too.' Then he lay back and looked up at the early summer sky through the young leaves of the silver birches which had sprung up to replace the fallen oaks. It was so clear and blue up there it could have been the sky in Methwin's World. But it wasn't.

In the distance a sharp, coughing bark was answered by another. Matt sat up suddenly. 'Foxes!' he uttered, in awe.

'Do you think they'll come to Foxdown Wood?' Cathy's eyes sparkled at the thought.

'Not while the digging is going on, but maybe in a month or two. The young ones will be looking for new territories before winter, and there are plenty of good places to dig earths here. We might be lucky.'

Cathy hugged her knees and looked out dreamily over the soft, rolling landscape of the chalk hills. 'I'd like that and I'm sure Vix would, too.'

There was silence for a few moments as Matt scoured the landscape, hoping for a flash of russet-brown fur running along the edge of the wood beyond the next field.

'Guess what?' he said at last.

'What?'

'Dad's promised to get me a dog from the RSPCA on Saturday. Want to come and help me choose?'

All Lion books are available from
your local bookshop, or can be ordered
direct from Lion Publishing. For a free
catalogue, showing the complete list of
titles available, please contact:

Customer Services Department
Lion Publishing plc
Peter's Way
Sandy Lane West
Oxford OX4 5HG

Tel: (01865) 747550
Fax: (01865) 715152